Under the laws of the Nine-Star League, all men are slaves. But when Soleyla Devarian, a captain of the elite League Guardians, falls in love with her new pleasure slave, Kantou, she begins to question the very League she is sworn to uphold.

Badly abused by his previous owner, Kantou is handsome, intelligent, and painfully vulnerable. Soleyla, moved by his yearning for a woman to whom he can give himself utterly, vows to prove she is that woman, and to make Kantou feel safe enough to submit to her completely.

But when she is posted to Antoros, a newly discovered world in the far reaches of the galaxy, Soleyla finds herself equally drawn to Rolen, the fiery, passionate leader of the Antorean rebels the Guardians have been ordered to crush. Now Soleyla is trapped between two alluring men and their conflicting desires, and there's only one way to fulfill them both!

WARNING: This book contains explicit sexuality, anal penetration, m/m/f ménage scenes, and voyeurism.

This book was previously published many years ago and has been reedited for its rerelease.

REVIEWS

2006 CAPA Nominee! Best BDSM

A Love Romances & More Staff Pick! "An exciting and extremely erotic new trilogy."

A Road to Romance Recommended Read! "A wild, edge of the seat ride! This is truly one of those rare books you cannot put down."

5 Blue Ribbons! "Beautifully crafted, erotic, and passionate . . . If you are new to erotic romance, then DEVARIAN EXILE is an excellent starting point. And for those devotees of erotic romance amongst you, I would say that if you miss this book, you do so at your own peril." Romance Junkies

5 Stars! "A sexy, seductive and romantic science fiction tale that I could not put down!" Just Erotic Romance Reviews

5 Flags! "This book is so hot it must NOT be read without access to air conditioning, a bucket of ice, and a cold shower!" Euro-Reviews

DEVARIAN EXILE
DEVARIAN CHRONICLES 1

BY

SIERRA DAFOE

Devarian Exile
Copyright © 2023 Sierra Dafoe
ISBN: 978-1-4874-3930-9
Cover art by Martine Jardin

Published by eXtasy Books Inc

Look for us online at:
www.eXtasybooks.com

CHAPTER ONE

Captain Soleyla Devarian strode through the market, her blue Guardian's cloak whipping behind her, rage blazing through every sinew of her body. How *dare* her mother do this to her? She was so furious she spared barely a glance for the tents she passed, or even for the slaves displayed outside them.

If she was going to be forced to spend six months on some barren mudball halfway across the galaxy, Soleyla swore to herself, she was damned if she was going to spend it alone.

The first time she'd seen the market on Porto V, Soleyla had been sixteen. For the daughters of senators, the purchase of one's first pleasure slave was as much a rite of passage as the sword trial itself. The trial, a culmination of three years' military training in the Guardian schools, was both final exam and placement test. When Soleyla had disarmed the three V'ranyii her sword mistress sent against her in record time, slaying two in the process and simultaneously earning herself a Guardian commission as a second lieutenant, her mother had rewarded her in the customary manner by ordering the portals readied for the journey to Porto.

From the biting cold of an Argulian winter, Soleyla had stepped from the portal onto soft white sand. The feathery fronds of unfamiliar trees had rustled in a light, warm breeze. Wide-eyed, she'd followed her mother from the debarkation point down the slope toward the market.

The colored awnings and silken tents had looked flimsy to Soleyla, raised as she was on Argulus where the fierce winter

1

winds necessitated massive stone buildings to withstand their blast. The market had spread out before her, a riot of color under a gentle yellow sun. But it wasn't the tents, or even the azure sea sparkling off in the distance, that caught Soleyla's eye.

It was the men.

They'd posed outside the sellers' tents, living advertise-ments of their owners' wares. Their firm, taut bodies reignited the strange, unfamiliar restlessness that had begun plaguing her over the past few months, swelling the pulsing heat be-tween her legs. Soleyla had studied them, following the line of their taut, tapered waists to where their greatest assets were displayed to her devouring gaze, nestled amid curls of black, brown, or copper hair.

One slave, a sleek, light-haired fellow with eyes the color of the distant sea, had fondled himself before her eyes, his cock hardening under his caressing fingers as he shot Soleyla a beckoning, seductive glance.

Her mouth had gone dry as she stared at his hands trailing up and down his thickening shaft. She'd watched him rub the darkening tip between his deft fingers, stroking them lightly across the velvety skin. Her footsteps lagged, and she'd found herself wanting to command him to rub himself faster, want-ing to watch the muscles of his forearm clench and flex as he tightened his grip, watch his head drop back and his eyes fall shut as he stroked his warm, pulsing erection harder and harder . . .

Rachel Devarian had looked down at her flushed, staring daughter with an amused smile. "Patience, Soleyla," she'd murmured. "Do you think the merchants put their best wares on display in the streets?"

Obediently, Soleyla had followed her red-cloaked mother, but she hadn't been able to resist glancing back at the light-haired man, catching an expression of disappointment on his

2

face as the tall, regal woman, clearly marked by her crimson cloak with its titanium clasp as a Senator of the Nine-Star League, moved away.

It hadn't been likely that the man—a mere pleasure slave—had known her mother's name, much less her preeminence as First Senator of the League. But that hardly mattered, Soleyla had realized, watching the way his eyes followed Rachel. A forlorn hope shone in them, and she could almost read his thoughts. To be plucked from the pleasure market, taken into the household of a senator! It would be the height of ambition for slaves such as these—men selected in childhood for their attractiveness and trained in the arts of pleasing a woman.

It had never occurred to her that men had dreams, too—no matter how small and inconsequential those dreams might seem to her, Soleyla, daughter of Senator Rachel Devarian, Regent of Argulus IV.

She hadn't been entirely ignorant, of course, of the sensual uses to which a man could be put, even at sixteen. She'd walked in on her mother and one or more of the six pleasure slaves her rank entitled her to, any number of times. But she herself had had no more than the briefest of conversations with the ordinary slaves who tended the fields, the manor, the livestock—and none at all with the six her mother kept for pleasure.

It had been a shock to realize they might have dreams.

Her mother had led her to Merkun's establishment—an interlocking series of blue silken tents, the fabric fluttering lightly in the soft, sultry breeze. Wave after wave of half-understood sensation had flowed through her as Merkun paraded one man after another through the small blue chamber. Soleyla had watched Rachel inspect the men, her mother's long, capable fingers feeling their muscles, caressing their buttocks, curving down to cup their full, heavy testes. Soleyla had longed to be the one touching them, caressing all that

3

warm, waiting flesh, but she'd sat quietly, awaiting her mother's choice.

Finally, her mother had decided on Danel. Dear, sweet Danel, who'd eased her gently into the knowledge of her own womanhood, who'd always been there, eager to please, whenever she'd wanted him. His softness, his sweetness, his gentle pliancy to her moods and needs had made him, Soleyla had to admit, an ideal selection for her first pleasure slave.

Which made her mother's betrayal bitter indeed.

That first trip to Porto had been six years ago. Now, at twenty-two, Soleyla was far more versant with the emotions that tumbled through her at the sight of those hard, chiseled bodies so delectably displayed before her. The hunger she'd ruthlessly suppressed over the three months since her mother's betrayal roared through her as they preened, their poses and gestures and soft seductive looks all for her this time. But desire reminded her fiercely of Danel and so fueled her rage, keeping her firmly on her course toward Merkun's blue tent.

Her mother had been right about many things, including the preeminence of Merkun's establishment. That thought, too, carried its own weight of fury.

Merkun smiled and bowed as she entered his voluminous, multi-roomed tent. He had been castrated when granted his freedom by the regent of Porto V in token of fifteen years of outstanding service. Now the fat, aging man taught the extraordinary skills which had won him his freedom to the men he groomed for sale—one of the many reasons Merkun's pleasure slaves commanded such outrageous prices.

As he ushered her into the same small room she'd sat in six years before, Soleyla was surprised by a sharp stab of grief. Here, she'd sat here on this very chair, the first time she'd seen Danel. His soft hazel eyes had studied her quietly as her mother inspected him, tilted his neck, felt his buttocks and genitals. Soleyla shut her own eyes tightly against the memory of his warm, gentle gaze.

"Captain? Are you all right, my lady?"

She opened her eyes again. "Yes. Some wine, I think, Merkun."

He gestured to one of the two young men standing near the curtain that gave the room privacy. They were hardly more than boys, both of them, lean-limbed and beautiful. Merkun's future stock, being assiduously groomed for their duties. The youth came forward, comfortable in his nudity, and knelt gracefully beside her to pour the wine. Merkun took a seat across from her and smiled approvingly as the youth held the cup up to her, his eyes cast demurely downward.

"Would my lady care for anything else?"

She shook her head and waved him away. Merkun leaned forward, waiting — it was not his place to begin business, but hers.

It had been three months. Whatever grief she still felt, it was time for a new slave. Soleyla cleared her throat harshly.

"I'm being sent to Antoros. You've heard, of course."

Merkun inclined his head.

Of course he had heard. Everyone had. It was tantamount to exile, being posted to that newly discovered world in the far reaches of the galaxy. And for a regent to send her own daughter to such a place . . . It took Soleyla a moment to push back her bitterness enough to continue.

"I'll need a new slave. I'll be damned if I'm going to that obscure rock-heap without one."

"Of course, Guardian. Do you have any special requirements?"

Soleyla nodded. "He'll need to be more than simply a pleasure slave. The situation requires it. I can't have a pretty thing with no common sense. He's got to be tough, and willing to do manual labor, if needed." She stared at Merkun challengingly. Slaves, of course, could be commanded to do anything, but pleasure slaves held an exalted status.

The old man nodded. "I understand. It's an outpost. Of course you can't take a pampered lapdog."

"I'd prefer him reasonably bright, as well as biddable. I don't need to worry about his primary skills, seeing as he comes from your hands."

Merkun smiled acknowledgement of the praise. "I believe I have a few who might suit, Guardian. If you'll wait a moment?"

She nodded, and again Merkun gestured to the youths by the curtain, indicating they should entertain her as he slipped out.

Soleyla leaned back, feeling the rage that had carried her here seep away, leaving behind an enervating melancholy. The two youths moved around her, setting a bowl of chilled fruit close to hand, refilling her wine. One settled on a cushion in the corner and picked up a syrinka, plucking a soft, melancholy tune from its four strings. The melody made sharp tears prickle behind her eyelids.

Danel, too, had played the syrinka.

"Leave me," she ordered. The youths glanced at each other, panic flickering in their eyes.

"My lady?"

She softened her tone. "Don't worry. You've served well. But I wish solitude."

"Of course, my lady." Bowing, they withdrew, and Soleyla sank gratefully into the privacy of her grief.

Oh, Danel.

How clearly she remembered the feel of his hands, kneading the tension from the back of her neck, the slight hesitation he always made before sliding them downward to play over her generous breasts—a hesitation, she knew, calculated to give her time to indicate her desires without saying a word.

If she straightened under his touch, he knew that she did not wish his attentions, and tactfully withdrew. If she sighed and leaned back into his caresses, that was his cue to move his strong fingers down over her large, firm mounds, rubbing her hardening nipples. When she arched her back, he'd move to kneel before her, closing his lips firmly around one taut areola, drawing it into his mouth and suckling it.

She loved the ache that spread through her at the feel of his warm mouth pulling at her nipples. He'd lap at one breast, then the other, moving his mouth back and forth between them like a puppy seeking the teat, rasping his tongue over the hard, rosy nubs till they stood as erect as his cock, which brushed undemandingly against her thigh.

Under his ministrations, her breasts — which had reached their full size only in the past two years — had seemed to swell even more, pressing against his teasing hands. She'd arch still further, letting him devour them, shuddering at the soft scrape of his teeth across her nipples, feeling his cock pulsing against her but ignoring it in the ecstasy of his mouth tugging at her breasts. Often she'd keep him there, her fingers twined deep in his thick, soft hair, while the ache inside her built and built until it exploded in liquid heat between her thighs.

Sweet, gentle Danel.

Soleyla heard the rustle of silk and opened her eyes. Horrified to discover there were tears on her cheeks, she hastily wiped them away, glad that the slave who'd entered through the curtain had his eyes cast properly downward. Merkun followed, lingering long enough to register her nod of approval. Soleyla waved him back out and looked the slave over.

He was sturdily built, with neither the overdeveloped muscles of the showier slaves nor the ethereal beauty the two youths had possessed. His eyes were a pleasant, clear brown, and he looked capable enough. Soleyla stood and walked slowly around him.

Thick honey-colored hair, broad shoulders, good firm ass. She laid her hand flat on his chest and ran it downward, feeling him relax into her touch. His penis stirred and lengthened, displaying a nice, full cockhead, but . . .

Resuming her seat, she studied him, considering. Was it simply the memory of Danel that was blocking her own arousal? This one was handsome enough, certainly, and his quick brown eyes promised a good degree of intelligence, yet . . .

"Come," she said, and unclasped her blue Guardian's mantle. He knelt before her, his fingers deftly undoing the buttons of her shirt. Soleyla watched his eyes widen appreciatively as he uncovered her breasts. They were, she had to admit, exceptional—large and firm, with high, hard nipples. The slave stared at them, entranced. Then, glancing up at her for permission, he cupped his hands around their lush roundness.

Soleyla watched his eyes turn a deeper, glowing brown at the feel of her breasts overflowing his hands. His cock sprung fully erect, twitching lightly in its eagerness—but she herself felt nothing. Abruptly, she sat back. "Leave me."

He rose fluidly, his chin dropping to his chest in mortification, and disappeared through the curtain. Soleyla pulled her shirt closed but didn't bother to button it as Merkun entered. "He was displeasing, my lady?"

Soleyla shook her head. "He was fine. He just . . ."

He just wasn't Danel.

Something flickered in Merkun's eyes. It might have been compassion. The old man's voice was husky with an emotion Soleyla couldn't identify. "Skills can be taught. Techniques can be learned. But if the fit isn't right—"

"Yes," she replied, too quickly. "Precisely. He wasn't the right fit."

Merkun was silent a moment. Then, hesitantly, he said, "There is one in my stock who . . . I have no particular reason to think he'd be suitable, you understand, although he's certainly bright enough. But intuition, if you will allow an old man his follies, tells me he might be worth your consideration."

Soleyla eyed him. "Why the hesitation, Merkun? What aren't you telling me?"

"He's been . . . damaged, my lady."

"Damaged how?"

The old man shook his head. "I have been in this business all my life, first as a pleasure slave myself, and then as a seller. And in all that time I have never seen a slave—" He stopped speaking abruptly, as if words had failed him. "I bought him back. I had to. When I saw what had been done to him . . . My lady, I have never once had a complaint about a slave I sold. Until this one. And frankly . . ."

He glanced at her. His tone dropped to a whisper, as if he were terrified of what he was about to say.

As well he might be, she thought as he concluded, "I don't think the fault was on the slave's part."

Soleyla sipped her wine, studying him. "If I were my mother, Merkun, those words would have cost you your life."

"But you are not your mother, my lady."

Soleyla met his eyes. What she saw there surprised her. There was pride in his steady regard, a pride as great as any senator's. What right had an ex-slave to be so proud? She was tempted to ask him, but there was something more there as well. There was judgment. A keen, fierce intelligence that had weighed Rachel Devarian—and found her lacking.

Soleyla sat back. "Bring him, then." Merkun nodded and rose. She stopped him just before he disappeared through the curtain. "What's his name?"

"Kantou," he replied. He bowed briefly and left.

CHAPTER TWO

Kantou. She liked the sound of it. It had a lazy, playful, sensuous lilt that appealed to her.

Soleyla bit into a slice of chilled melon, enjoying the sweet crispness of the cool fruit as she imagined what this Kantou might look like. Idly, she reached for her wineglass and discovered a man kneeling before her, holding it out. He'd entered so quietly she hadn't even heard him.

His head was bent low, his eyes hidden behind a fall of gleaming ash-brown hair. His fingers around the carved crystal were long and slender — an artist's hands, or a musician's. That in turn reminded her of Danel, and for a moment Soleyla wondered what she was doing here, why she was even bothering. Then Kantou tilted his chin up, revealing broad, high cheekbones and a full, sensuous mouth.

Soleyla slid her hand underneath his chin, raising it higher, and found herself looking into eyes the color of an Argulian storm.

He's been . . . damaged, my lady.

There were shadows in Kantou's smoky gray eyes, dark shadows. But his expression remained calm, undemanding, and the shadows stayed far back where she could not read them. She saw intelligence clearly, however, in the shift and play of thoughts within those eyes.

What did he hope for, she wondered — did he still hope for anything?

His body was lean, the bulge of his deltoids well defined, and the strong neck muscles showed clearly as he knelt before

10

her. His belly was flat, rippled slightly, and she could see a soft trail of hair leading from the dip of his navel down to his groin. He waited, unmoving, under her scrutiny. She reached out her hand for the glass. As she took it, her fingers brushed his lightly, and she felt a quiver deep inside her.

Yes, this one was definitely worth considering.

"Thank you, Kantou. You may stand now. There." She gestured to the center of the room. Obediently, Kantou stood and backed up to the spot she'd indicated. He waited diffidently, his eyes on the floor.

Soleyla sipped her wine slowly, and just as slowly looked him over, savoring both.

He might have been a statue, so still he stood. He was perfectly proportioned, his body tapering from strong, muscled shoulders through narrow waist and hips to long, powerful thighs. Runner's thighs. He might be three or four years older than she, perhaps—or maybe it was just his stillness that made her think so. He gave an impression of patience, endurance—something deep and inherently unbreakable.

Unbreakable. What an odd word to think about a slave! For all that they were property, men were still human and treated as such. They were clothed, fed, educated to a suitable level, and treated with a relative degree of affection. 'The slave reflects the mistress' was an old, old adage, one Soleyla had heard many times. Breaking a slave, or even trying to, had never entered her mind.

She stood, feeling her shirt fall open again. The slave didn't glance up as she approached, though he must, surely he *must* see her breasts, freely exposed to the small, silent room. She came closer, standing before him so that those dark, haunting eyes were now gazing directly down at her open shirt. Still he betrayed no reaction.

Soleyla placed her hands on his chest, feeling the fine sprinkling of hair beneath her palms, enjoying the warm, smooth skin. She slid her hands downward, noting the curve of his ribcage, the firm bands of muscle across his abdomen, then let her fingers trail along the solid, narrow hipbones and brush quickly over his crotch. The hair there was brown as well, almost silky. He had a crisp, pleasant scent to him, like just-melted snow. Cupping his balls lightly, Soleyla let the weight of them rest against her palm. She squeezed them together, reveling in their size, their firmness. Held together like that, they overflowed her hand.

A stab of heat shot through her belly as she looked at his penis. Even flaccid, she could tell it was larger than Danel's. *How much larger?* she wondered with a quickening pulse. She stroked a deft finger over the sensitive skin just behind his scrotum, and was rewarded with a brief, barely controlled quiver.

She studied his face, bent before hers — without her boots on, she calculated he'd be a scant inch or two taller than her. For now, she enjoyed the slight down-tilt of his chin, the straight, well-shaped nose, the dark lashes shading his eyes — which were, she smiled to herself, now fixed on her breasts.

Playfully, she spread her shirt wider, baring them fully. They stood out like melons, generously round, tingling under her touch as she trailed her fingers over them, following their swelling curves down into the warm hollow between, then cupped her palms underneath and lifted them toward his gaze. His lips, she saw, had parted just slightly, and his eyes glittered under those long dark lashes. She ran her thumbs slowly up the outer curve of her breasts, then brought her fingers together, trapping the nipples. Rubbing them, she felt them harden under her touch, and glanced down to see Kantou's cock lengthening.

Definitely larger than Danel's. She gave a throaty chuckle and tugged her nipples lightly, watching his reaction. "Does that please you, Kantou?"

She felt, rather than saw, his back stiffen. The glitter in his eyes disappeared. Carefully, he replied, "If it pleases you, my lady."

Damn! Soleyla stepped back. Here she was, almost aching to have this slave touch her, and he'd retreated into cold, careful formality. She could command him, of course . . .

Instead, she continued her perusal, circling him—and gasped at the scars that laced his broad back.

They were knotted, overlaid, as if whoever had beaten him hadn't waited for them to heal before whipping him again. Soleyla felt a wave of rage so fierce it almost made her nauseous. No one—not anyone—should whip a dog that way, much less a slave. She strode back to face Kantou, and yanked his chin up so he was forced to look up at her.

"Who did that to you?"

He regarded her warily. "My former mistress, my lady. I . . . failed to please."

"How?"

He looked away.

"How, Kantou?"

He shrugged. "She didn't care for my attitude, my lady."

"I see." And Soleyla did. That cautious, controlled exterior of his . . . Yes, by the right—or wrong—sort of woman, his stiff self-possession could be viewed as an insult. Such things had been known to happen.

Her body was thrumming with a hunger deeper than she'd felt in months, but she pushed it aside. Antoros was no glory posting. It was a rough, just-discovered frontier planet, years or even decades away from being brought into the League. Soleyla had no illusions as to why she was being sent there. It was banishment, pure and simple—a not-so-subtle reminder of who, between herself and her mother, held the power. Soleyla grimaced.

She'd need more than a play toy in that environment. And certainly not an unwilling one. Abruptly, she made her decision. "Kantou!" He looked up, those keen gray eyes studying her. "I will not purchase you if you do not want." His eyes widened in surprise at her words. She was offering him a choice. Slaves were not offered choices. Soleyla continued, "I will have you willing, Kantou, or not at all. But make no mistake—if I buy you, I *will* have you. Where, when, and as I like."

His eyes darkened again. Soleyla turned away, strode back to her chair, and waited, feigning indifference, for him to mull it over. She toyed with the fruit, poured herself some more wine. Felt the friction of her shirt rubbing against her hard nipples. And waited some more.

Finally, she looked at him. He was staring at her, a strange, hollow hunger in his eyes. He looked like a frightened, starving dog.

"Will you beat me?"

"Never." And she meant it. If she couldn't handle a slave without resorting to violence . . ."But I *will* expect you to obey me, Kantou. Immediately and without question."

Nervously, he jerked his head in acquiescence. She studied him again, that lean, firm body, that luscious ash-brown hair . . . A hunger of her own, denied now for months, roared inside her, demanding satisfaction.

"All well and good," she said. "But I'm going to give you a chance to prove it—and a chance, too, to discover if obeying me will be too much of a trial. Now . . ."

Soleyla considered for a moment, then smiled, thinking of that day long ago when her mother first brought her to Porto. Remembering the sleek, golden-haired slave who'd fondled himself, trying to entice her. It had never occurred to her to have Danel fulfill *that* particular fantasy.

But Kantou would. Right now.

Soleyla leaned back in the oversized chair and waved a languid hand. "Play with yourself, slave. I want to watch."

Slowly, his dark, shadowed eyes fixed on hers, Kantou slid his hand down to his cock. His very unwillingness was strangely arousing, and Soleyla felt for the first time a pure erotic pleasure in the power itself, the power to make this man do whatever she wanted — whether he was willing or not. But by the end, she swore, he'd be willing — more than willing. She smiled again.

"Come closer, Kantou." He approached until he was a scant four feet away from her. From her chair, she had an excellent view. "Now touch yourself, lightly."

His cock was already half-hard, she saw, the veins starting to swell along its length. In light of its considerable size now, she could barely wait to see it fully erect.

Faithful to her command, he stroked one finger lightly down the length of his shaft. It leapt under his touch like an overeager mount, thickening rapidly. Soleyla licked her lips and leaned forward, watching.

"Good, that's good. Now stroke the head. Just the head."

Gritting his teeth, Kantou ran his fingertip around the thick, meaty rim, fighting the instinctive urge to wrap his hand around his shaft and pump. Electric tingles spread down his shaft and into his balls at that whispery touch. It was almost as if someone else was touching him.

In a way, he thought, someone else was.

At her nod, he caressed the head again, then followed her command to put his finger in his mouth and moisten it. As he did so, he realized he was salivating freely. How was this woman making him so horny? His finger gleamed with saliva as he brought it back to his cock.

"Good. Now do it again."

For a third time he traced a circle around the rim of the head, tickling the underside of its lip, quivering at the smooth, wet caress of his finger. He groaned, deep in his throat. The woman's eyes gleamed brighter.

He was fully erect now, harder than he had been since . . . he wouldn't think of that. Not now. Not with his new mistress watching him, watching his hand . . .

His cock was so hard the skin gleamed, the slit in the tip spread wide by the swelling. It gaped like a small, hungry mouth, a pearl of pre-cum already gleaming at the opening.

"Rub it in. Just the head!" she commanded sharply as his hand automatically started to close around his shaft. Fighting for control, Kantou placed his finger against that small, gaping hole, rubbing lightly, then flicking his finger back and forth over it, gasping at the sensation. When he saw her vision fixed on his frantic rubbing, he pressed harder, working the moist, slippery stuff down the curve of the head, around the sensitive rim, being careful not to brush the shaft. He moaned as he did so, his hips jerking involuntarily. Another pearly drop of juice slid from his slit. The head of his cock was so sensitive he could feel the drop sliding over his skin.

"Again."

He almost wanted to weep with desire but, ignoring the throbbing of his shaft and the thick, heavy ache building up in his balls, he steadied his hand, touched it lightly to the fresh bead of cum, and smeared it over the enlarged, purple head of his cock, pinching it lightly, then harder, shuddering with an unfulfilled ache. His balls swelled painfully, screaming for release.

Almost as if she'd heard him, his new mistress tilted her head back, a wicked smile playing about her lips as he stood there, helpless, his body aching with need.

"Not yet," she commanded. "Spread it open."

Instinctively, he knew what she wanted, and pushed his

fingers down the sides of the tip, making his slit gape even wider. He stood, head down, cumhole spread wide for her inspection.

Kantou felt as if he'd been pinioned on thin air, lacerated by the dual demands of his desire and the need to control it. Quivering, he struggled to keep his hands from his throbbing shaft, trying desperately to wait for her next command as she leaned forward, studying his cock. He heard sounds escape him and realized he was begging.

"Please, please . . ."

"All right." She nodded and sat back, her breasts thrusting out of her half-open shirt. Only the high flush dotting her cheekbones and the deepening color of her nipples betrayed her sensations. He would do almost anything to taste those long, hard nubs, to suck them into his mouth and flick them with his tongue . . . Gratefully, he slid one hand around the shaft of his cock, squeezing it.

"No! Lightly, Kantou."

He almost whimpered. *How is she doing this to me?* he wondered with some half-obliterated part of his brain. *She commands, and I ache to obey. Why could the last one not do this to me?* Gently, he pressed down on his cock, feeling the taut skin slide under his grip. The veins in his shaft throbbed at the touch. His balls ached painfully. Grimly, he ignored them, and concentrated on keeping his touch light when everything inside him wanted to clamp down on it, pull the skin faster, harder . . .

"Good!"

At her praise, a sense of accomplishment filled him. He'd pleased her. He held his hand still, waiting for her next order, feeling cum leaking steadily from the tip.

Soleyla was hornier than she'd ever been. She didn't dare touch herself, didn't even dare shift in her seat. The second she did, she knew, she'd peak. And she didn't want to. She wanted to make this last forever, wanted to keep him at that incredible pitch for hours, days . . . There had to be a way to increase the intensity somehow, without letting him come.

She could feel her own need rising, the lips of her pussy growing thick and damp, aching to be probed. But how could she command this slave if she couldn't command herself? She forced her passion down, feeling it both contract and grow stronger. Leaning forward, she blew gently on that luscious, gleaming cockhead, and heard him gasp with sensation. His penis flexed beneath his restraining fingers, and she could see him fighting for control.

"Does that please you, Kantou?"

"Yes, my lady." *No more of this 'if it pleases you' crap*, she thought with satisfaction.

She glanced up at his heavy, half-closed eyes. "Will you do whatever I tell you, Kantou?"

"Yes, my lady." His voice was rough with barely controlled need.

"You had pain, before, from the last one," she said. It wasn't a question. His eyes opened a slit, though his huge erection, she saw, still pulsed as hard as ever. "Tell me, Kantou, did she ever at least turn the pain into pleasure?"

He shook his head mutely, the shadows back in his eyes. *Damn.*

"Stroke it slowly, Kantou." Soleyla spoke gently and watched as he closed his eyes, letting his hand close firmly around his cock. His flesh swelled around the tightness of his grip, and Soleyla's breath caught in her throat. "That's right, squeeze it harder. But slowly. Slowly, my beauty."

His face went slack, half in ecstasy, half in stark need, as his fist squeezed his shaft, the head swelling above it. He moved his hand up and down with agonizing slowness. "Harder," she breathed, feeling her own need rising swiftly. He squeezed harder, grabbing his cock in a stranglehold, and moaned through his teeth.

"Does it hurt?" she asked softly.

"Yes, my lady. It hurts."

"Does it feel good, Kantou?"

He replied with a deep, sensual groan. She could see his balls, full and tight against the base of his shaft, unbelievably hard. His right hand moved slowly, caressing his cock as she commanded, and gently she took his left hand in hers, cupping it over his testes. "Rub them, Kantou." His hand closed over them, moving in a slow, circular motion. Soleyla watched, her breath tightening. "Now squeeze them." He did, and she saw his cock throb in reaction.

He was helpless now, trapped in the grip of his need, his right hand stroking his cock with a steady, excruciating slowness while with his left he squeezed and tugged at his balls. Soleyla imagined those hands on her breasts and felt a fresh spurt of wetness between her legs. "Harder," she said. He clamped his hand tighter, moaning with mingled pain and desire.

Juice spilled from the tip of his cock in a steady trickle. She commanded him to spread it down over himself, and watched avidly as his fingers, slick with cum, slid over his deep purple shaft. She was going to come, just watching him. So she finally did what she'd wanted to do since the day she'd first come to Porto. She drew him beside her and whispered, "Harder, Kantou. Harder and faster, my beauty, my pet, make it sting . . ."

Soleyla watched the muscles bunching in his arms as he savaged his cock, letting go of his balls to wrap both hands around the huge, thick, impossibly swollen shaft, pistoning the skin up and down at her panted orders. She rocked in her chair, willing him on, reaching out to let his hard, aching balls rub against her palm.

"Please," she heard him whisper as he tilted his hips

forward, pushing his balls against her hand. Fulfilling his newfound need, she closed her fingers around them and squeezed.

"Yes," he breathed. "Oh, mistress, please!"

She clamped her hand down, crushing them together, and felt them tighten even further as his shaft bucked and jerked and his slit gaped wide, pulsating.

Soleyla felt her own orgasm start as he came, his semen streaming like tickertape into the air and across her swollen breasts. As she arched her back up to greet it, he collapsed to his knees. Clamping his hands around her aching breasts, he sucked them like a starving man, and she closed her eyes as the world exploded into bright waves of fire.

CHAPTER THREE

L ater, after she'd made him lick every drop of his cum from her breasts, Soleyla allowed Kantou to curl at her feet, his head resting wearily against her firm thigh. Her fingers played softly through his long hair, and she could see the ugly scars lacing his back. The sight of them raised a fierce protectiveness within her, a strange, novel sensation. With Danel, if anything, it had been the other way around—it had been he who had looked after *her*, teaching her, gently fulfilling the desires she hadn't known yet how to convey.

She'd been a girl, then, with a girl's needs and feelings. Now she was a woman, and she knew what she wanted.

And Kantou belonged to her in a way Danel never had. Danel had been her mother's gift, a reward for passing the sword trial—a gift Rachel had callously ripped away the moment her daughter defied her.

No one would take Kantou away. Ever. Soleyla felt the heavy bulge of the coin purse at her waist. He would truly be the first that belonged to her. But her ownership of him ran deeper than money. She had, she sensed, made him truly hers—hers to command in every act, every motion. Every pleasure he felt would be at her orders.

She glanced again at the hideous scars marring his smooth muscled back. Who could have done such a thing?

She'd better not find out, she cursed silently. If she learned who had done that to her Kantou . . .

Her Kantou. The words made her smile. As if in response, he tilted his head on her knee and looked up at her. The gray eyes were clearer now, the shadows momentarily dissipated. Someday, she swore, they would be gone forever.

He studied her somberly, his eyes luminous and vulnerable with the unexpected renewal of hope. "May I ask you something, my lady?"

She brushed his long hair back from his smooth, high forehead. "What is it, Kantou?"

His eyes dropped modestly. "Was it . . . like that before, with the others?"

"There was only one other before you, Kantou. And no, it wasn't like that."

"I . . . I wanted so much to please you, and yet I barely even touched you . . ."

"You did," Soleyla replied, stroking his hair. "You pleased me very much. There will be plenty of time to please me in other ways."

With a small, relieved sigh, he dropped his head back to her knee, like a weary traveler who'd found, at last, a haven.

That was how Merkun found them when he scratched discreetly for admittance. He peered closely at Kantou, curled at her feet as if nestling into the refuge of her protection.

Soleyla smiled at Merkun—it was hard not to like a man who so obviously cared about the slaves he trained and sold. "As you see, this one suits me well, Merkun." She rose gracefully, unhooked her coin purse from her belt, and tossed it to him. "Take what you will for him."

He smiled back and gave a slight bow. "It is a pleasure doing business with you, Guardian Devarian."

His smile froze at a small harsh noise from Kantou. Soleyla turned to see her new slave suddenly crouched by the chair, a look of stark terror on his face.

"Kantou, what is it?" She moved toward him, but he recoiled, staring at her, his eyes suddenly black with fear. "Kantou!"

Soleyla spun to Merkun, her fierce gaze demanding an explanation. Merkun was standing, his mouth half-open, his face pale.

"Stupid, stupid . . . My lady, I said your name."

Soleyla stared at him. "And?"

The old man bowed his head. "The lady who first bought him, the lady who—"

"Beat him. Yes." Soleyla cut him off impatiently. Behind her, she could hear Kantou's panicked breathing. She could gladly kill the woman who had reduced him to this.

Merkun paused. He looked down, his voice falling to a whisper. "You are *not* your mother, my lady. I'd hoped Kantou would see that."

Soleyla's eyes widened with sudden comprehension and her fury narrowed to a sharp, deadly point. Merkun held out the coin purse, his old face regretful. "I am sorry. I presumed too far."

Soleyla stared at the coins in his hand, then looked at Kantou. He watched her like a wary, frightened animal. Enraged, she slapped the offered coins to the ground.

"You are right, Merkun. I'm not my mother. Leave us." The old man hesitated. "Leave us!"

He bowed, then withdrew. Soleyla turned back to Kantou, took a step toward him. He flinched. Softly, she spoke, her words firm and reassuring. "I told you, Kantou, no one will ever touch you again without my permission."

Shadows flickered in his eyes. Soleyla saw hope there, but also doubt—a doubt born of deep, remembered pain. She glanced around the small blue room, but there was nothing here that could help him—or her. She sighed, gestured gently. "Come, Kantou." Flinching, he followed her out of the tent.

As she came out into the bright sunshine of Porto, Soleyla felt her rage grow hard and adamant, remembering the tall, graceful woman who had walked beside her through this market, six years ago. She herself was now as tall, and equally graceful—but so very different in every other way from the cool, amused woman who'd looked down at her, smiling.

Rachel Devarian had much to account for.

Soleyla glanced back at the man following her, silent and afraid. "Have you been through a portal before, Kantou?"

He nodded cautiously, his face still pale with shock, and she studied him a moment, suddenly aware just how little she actually knew of him.

How much, for that matter, had she known of Danel? For almost six years he'd been her constant companion, there to soothe her tensions and give her pleasure. They'd talk, some-times—or rather *she* would, telling him about the training she was undergoing as a Guardian, and later about the raids and missions and skirmishes with the V'ranyii, her promotions, her frustrations, her ambitions. Danel would listen, those soft hazel eyes warm with interest, and rub her feet or her back. Later, after she'd said all she wanted, he would celebrate her triumphs or ease her frustrations with his tongue, his hands, his cock . . .

Had she ever truly known Danel? She'd never bothered to penetrate that calm, gentle surface—he was a pleasure slave, no more. There for *her* needs, *her* desires. She'd never both-ered to wonder if he had desires of his own.

And now she'd never know.

It would be different with Kantou, she swore. He'd shown a touching willingness to please her, willingness almost des-perate in its emotional need. Soleyla's anger flared again, but not at him. How could she blame him for that first, instinctive reaction? He'd shown nothing but a hunger to trust, so deep it was almost overpowering—until Merkun had blurted out her name.

He needed that, Soleyla realized. Having been so badly abused, something in Kantou desperately needed someone to trust. To belong to. Someone who could protect him, keep him safe. And the woman who'd offered him that had turned out to be Rachel Devarian's daughter.

Soleyla smiled at the irony, but there was no laughter in her. Not with those bleak shadows in her Kantou's eyes.

He stood silently, waiting for her orders, his gray eyes hidden again from her sight. Behind those stormy eyes lay a sharp intelligence, and an impressive self-control — and both were contained in a body more perfect than any she'd seen. He was truly exceptional — and now he was hers.

That knowledge brought a resurgence of heat to her loins, and she felt a slickness between her thighs. She remembered his hands, moving at her command over his huge, swollen cock, so much larger than Danel's had been. She was impatient to discover what it would feel like inside her. Impatient to have him as he'd been before, placing himself so trustingly in her care, bending that self-discipline to her every whim.

She *would* have that again, she swore silently. So would he. He hungered for it as deeply as she did, she suspected. But it would take time to pierce his rigid, guarded surface, to open him to her again as he'd been before. Time to allow him to see that Soleyla Devarian was not like her mother.

As she led Kantou to a weaver's stall to buy him raiment suitable for their destination, Soleyla smiled with a certain bitter amusement. It was ironic that the woman whose brutal abuse had created the need for that time was also the woman who'd guaranteed they would have it.

Time was the one thing they'd have no lack of, on Antoros.

CHAPTER FOUR

"Kantou, what are you doing?"

Kantou flinched at her words — sharper than she'd meant them to be — and almost dropped the delicate device he was holding.

Soleyla cursed inwardly. She *hated* it when he winced like that. For three solid weeks, they'd trekked through the trackless ridges of Antoros. Twenty-two days of solitude and silence, surrounded by jagged peaks that fell away unexpectedly to reveal vistas that left her breathless with their beauty — and still he would cringe if she startled him, or spoke too harshly.

And she'd just done both.

Soleyla sighed. It was getting harder and harder to be patient with him, and not simply because his jumpiness was beginning to wear on her. The continual presence of an attractive male — one she was determined not to touch until he was ready — was a constant, and unique, irritant.

Never before had she known what it meant to be frustrated in this manner. Since the first stirrings of her libido, sex had been something she'd taken as much for granted as air or food. Now the only thing standing between her and that lovely, chiseled body was her determination to prove to him that she was nothing like her prideful, vicious mother.

That determination, she had to admit, was wearing more and more thin with each day spent watching Kantou's long, muscled legs as he climbed ahead of her through these rough, untamed mountains. Her gaze devoured him as he squatted over their nightly campfire, preparing her meals. At night, he lay mere paces from her, his beautiful, chiseled face relaxed in the peace of sleep. Soleyla herself lay wakeful, listening to the silence of that vast and empty planet and feeling frustration coursing through her, throbbing between her thighs.

And the sight of him, hunkered shirtless in the afternoon heat, had almost shattered her resolve. She had just returned, sweaty and coated with grime, from the peak of whatever this particular brown heap of rocks was called. When she strode back into the small hollow where she'd left him, a stab of clamorous desire had bolted straight through her sore, tired body, setting her nerves to tingling and her teeth on edge.

Gritting back her frustration, Soleyla dropped her empty pack and squatted beside him. "It's all right, Kantou. But what are you doing with the tracker?"

As she looked closer, she saw he had the back casing off the instrument. If he'd dropped it in this sandy dirt . . . but he hadn't. Damn thing was half-useless, anyway. Its range simply wasn't up to this mountainous terrain, allowing them only occasional pings from the base camp, almost four hundred kilometers behind.

Commander Valda, a squarely built woman whose short silver hair clung to her head like a helmet, had turned down Soleyla's request for a flitter. She'd been barrack-mates with Soleyla's mother, years before, and Soleyla knew exactly whose will the commander was enforcing.

The entire company knew full well where the command for the famous Captain Soleyla Devarian's inclusion in the advance Antorean team had originated. Rank and file Guardians, with no family connections to keep them from such an unenviable posting, they'd stared when she'd arrived through the newly constructed portal — with a pleasure slave in tow, no less. Their dark, resentful expressions had made Soleyla just as glad to be assigned the menial, dirty — but

27

solitary—task of planting markers for the geodetic relay.

She was, she had to admit, rather looking forward to exploring the vast southern forests and open plains of this wild, undeveloped planet. But Commander Valda had insisted that planting markers in the range just north of the base camp had priority, and the flitters—so she claimed—couldn't handle the terrain.

It would have to be done—Valda had practically smirked—on foot.

Thus Soleyla's sigh as she sank down beside Kantou had as much to do with her very sore feet as it did with her sexual frustration. As if in apology for his instinctive reaction, Kantou held out the tracking device.

"I was trying to increase the range, my lady. I . . . I was very careful with it."

Soleyla tried to tear her attention from those bronzed, muscled arms long enough to study the tracker. The contrast between the strength of his body and the nervous vulnerability in his smoky gray eyes was disconcerting.

He's as strong as I am. The realization was a shock. *Stronger, even.*

But he was a man. A slave. For the first time, she wondered if the fact bothered him. *Of course it doesn't*, Soleyla told herself firmly. Men were born to slavery just as women were born to rule and provide for them. That was the way it had always been.

Except once, she remembered suddenly, it hadn't.

Soleyla pulled off a dusty boot, chasing away her disturbing ruminations. "Well, good," she said, shaking the collected sand and pebbles out of it. "That's good, Kantou."

He smiled in relief, and she leaned over to peer at the adjustments he'd made to the wiring. "Where'd you learn to do that?"

He shrugged. "The technicians at the child-house used to let me help them. I liked learning how things worked."

Replacing the casing carefully, he set the tracker aside and knelt before her to remove her other boot.

Soleyla groaned in relief as he worked his strong, capable fingers over the instep of her arch. His touch had other effects on her as well. But if she reached for him, she knew he'd only flinch as he'd done repeatedly over the past few weeks. Flinch, and then steel himself to suffer her commands.

Watching him force himself into submissive readiness had effectively dampened her ardor. No, damn it, she would have him willing!

She cast about for ways to distract herself from what his fingers, pressing into the balls of her foot, were doing to her.

"Where was your child-house, Kantou? Porto?"

He shook his head. "Marbul."

Marbul. A newer world of the League, wrested only thirty years previously from the V'ranyii. Soleyla tried to picture what it must have been like, growing up in one of the child-houses where male children were sent at birth. "You were there until you were what? Twelve?"

"That's the customary age, yes. At twelve they assess us for talents and abilities. I was placed with the others destined for the pleasure slave merchants."

"Not the technicians?"

Again, he shook his head. His gaze was distant, as if watching something she could not see. Something stirred in his eyes, a look of longing . . .

Soleyla gestured for the tracker and stood, feeling the warm, sandy dirt beneath her bare feet. He handed it to her, and she turned it on. The clear, strong ping of the signal was loud in the still mountain air.

She glanced down at him. Kantou dropped his gaze, reaching to retrieve her boots—but not before she'd seen a quick gleam of satisfaction in his eyes.

A sudden question occurred to her. "Would you have

preferred that, Kantou? To have been a work slave for the technicians, rather than a pleasure slave?"

The question was heresy. Kantou gave a quick, nervous glance around the rocky slope, even though they were obviously alone. They'd been alone for weeks. For the first time Soleyla understood just how deep his inhibitions, conditioned by centuries of custom — and punishment — ran.

"Kantou."

"My lady?"

His eyes had darkened to an inky charcoal precisely the color of Argulian storm clouds. Whatever thoughts he had were hidden effectively behind them.

"Answer me."

His mouth dropped open. He stammered a moment, then looked away and shrugged. Answer enough.

Soleyla studied his profile in the reddening light as he busied himself cleaning the dust from her boots. He was so beautiful, her Kantou. The idea of him castrated, as all males not destined for the pleasure-markets were, was more than she could stand.

"Put those aside," she commanded.

He set them down, then came and knelt before her at her signal. Soleyla felt her desire reawaken at the sight of his bent head, the shining ash-brown hair falling like a veil over his face. The hard nub of her sex swelled, pulsing. It was all she could do to keep herself from reaching out, burying her hand in that shining hair, and pulling his mouth firmly against that throbbing point . . .

Raising her head, she looked away from him, fighting down her lust. From here, the mountain range curved northward, then south again in the distance, cupping in its stony grasp a great open plain which was bathed now in long purple shadows. The far mountains were black against a sky streaked with riotous color.

For a moment, she forgot everything else in that glorious view. Her frustrations, her aches, the scratchy dirt on her skin. It was a beautiful planet, a new planet, fresh, unspoiled. A place of possibilities. And why shouldn't things be different, here on wild Antoros?

Soleyla smiled and looked down at Kantou. Gently, she tilted back his chin so that he looked up at her.

"You shall have both, Kantou. You have a mind, as well as a body. There's no reason you shouldn't learn whatever pleases you."

"My lady?"

The quick, frightened hope that gleamed in his eyes was almost painful to see. Moved by the strength of that long-hidden desire, Soleyla nodded. She would give that, and more, to see him happy. Her voice was husky with an emotion she could find no name for as she said, "You are more to me than just a pleasure slave, Kantou."

He paled with the strength of his emotions and closed his eyes. His head dropped back, exposing the long arch of his strong neck, letting the thick, shiny hair fall free. An evening breeze stirred it, and Soleyla felt her throat go dry. He knelt before her in a state almost of rapture, eyes closed, his face radiant, so moved was he by what she had offered. The shadows of dusk played across his clear, perfect skin, his cheekbones, the wide, sensuous curve of his mouth . . .

She could not stop herself. She bent and kissed those full, tender lips.

Automatically, he stiffened, his eyelids flying open. He almost jerked away from her touch before controlling himself with ruthless self-discipline.

Soleyla spun away. Rage and disappointment warred within her. Reaching for her boots, she stomped them on.

Kantou spoke behind her. "I'm sorry. It's just . . ." His voice dropped to a tormented whisper. "You look so like her, my lady."

She whipped around, stung by his words. Her hand rose to slap him. His eyes widened as he watched the blow coming.

She stopped it barely in time, clenched her fist shut, her nails digging into her palm. Horror and fury twisted together inside her.

Never, she'd promised. A promise she'd just nearly broken.

Gritting her teeth, she forced herself to look at him—and was shocked to see his hands at his waist, unbuckling his belt.

"Please, my lady . . ."

Her breath hissed through her teeth. Her eyes seemed trapped by those deft fingers, watching their every movement. Her throat ached with need.

"Kantou . . ." Her voice was almost a growl.

He raised a hand to her lips, stopped her protest. "You have been so patient with me. Please . . . do with me as you will."

Heat pounded in her groin, the product of weeks of frustration. He stepped back from her and stood, naked to the waist, his eyes fixed modestly on the ground as he awaited her pleasure. She could feel her hands cramp with the desire to wrap themselves around that warm, smooth skin, slide along the firmness of his muscles, close around the swelling of his cock and squeeze . . .

"Is this truly what you want, Kantou?"

He nodded but didn't raise his head. She stepped to him, caught his wrists, drew them away from his belt and placed her own hands there instead. Deftly, she loosened it and slid his pants downward, revealing that marvelously long penis, resting quietly against the hair of his groin.

Saliva flooded her mouth at the sight of it. She felt a corresponding spurt of wetness soak the lips of her sex. Running her tongue over her lips, she felt a strange, unfamiliar desire to take his cock in her mouth, taste the warm, silken length of it.

"Oh, Kantou," she breathed, and took his cock in her hands, feeling it start to thicken against her palm.

But when she looked in his eyes, she saw only apprehension.

Soleyla yanked her hand back and stalked away. She grabbed up her sword-belt, buckling it around her waist, seething at the heat pulsing between her thighs. How could she feel such unbridled desire, and this man — this slave! — feel nothing?

No. That was unfair. She knew it. He wanted to give himself to her — and was terrified of it at the same time.

Soleyla took a deep breath, checking her rage. She would accept no half-hearted submission. Nor would she blame him for a situation not of his making. She wanted him — wanted him so badly she could taste it — but she wanted him willing. More than willing. Eager. Aching to fulfill her every whim, as she ached to have him so . . .

She glanced back, saw him standing, a stricken look on his face. If she returned to him now, right now, there would be no drawing back. He would submit willingly, grateful for her forgiveness, thankful for whatever attentions she might choose to bestow . . .

Her own features felt cast of stone as she turned away. "Cover yourself, Kantou." Her voice was harsh against the soft Antorean night. "Prepare my dinner. I'll return for it later."

Ignoring the soft, ragged sound of his sob, she strode away into the darkness.

CHAPTER FIVE

Damn her mother!

Soleyla stomped loudly up the rise. It was ridiculous. Here she was, half a galaxy away from Argulus, and the woman was *still* controlling her life!

She climbed single-mindedly up the slope, feeling rage pulse like desire in her blood.

They'd never been close—but still the revelation of her mother's personality, written in scars across Kantou's back, had shocked Soleyla to the core. She should have guessed— she knew the brutality her mother was capable of, none better. It was Soleyla's refusal to match that single-minded drive that had cost her Danel. Her mother had taken him—sold him, most likely—and when Soleyla had furiously demanded to know his fate, her mother had smiled coldly and refused to answer.

Gritting her teeth, Soleyla pressed on.

What was it going to take to break through the barrier her mother's viciousness had erected inside Kantou? She had been patient with him, to a level unheard of with a slave. Now her entire body ached with an unslaked hunger, fierce and voracious. She didn't dare return to the hollow where they had camped in this mood. One glance at his prone, sleeping body, and the beast within her would break free of the tenuous hold she still retained on it.

Cursing viciously, she clambered her way to the top of the ridge, breathing heavily as she looked out over the moon-flooded plain below—and that was when a heavy hand closed around her throat.

"Do not reach for your weapon."

She froze in consternation. The voice was deep, rumbling. A man. A spurt of disbelieving rage raced through her. No man had ever dared lay a hand on her except at her command.

A renegade slave? She'd heard stories of such things, but here, on Antoros? Soleyla shifted, planting her feet firmly on the loose shale. The hand moved, sliding down to grip her arm, and something cold and sharp pressed against her neck.

A knife.

"What do you want?" she demanded. She felt him move behind her, and realized from the angle of his arm that her head was barely level with his shoulder.

"I might," he rumbled, "ask the same thing of you."

What? "Who are you? Release me this instant!"

The hand on her biceps tightened its grasp, pulling her against him. She could feel hard muscles against her back, could feel the warmth of him even through her leather shirt. He must be enormous.

"I think not, Guardian."

Soleyla stiffened at the title. He knew what she was, then — this wasn't an accidental meeting. His next words confirmed it.

"It's long I've been waiting to get my hands on one of you."

He was in for a shock if he thought a mere knife at her throat could hold her. Every woman — even the commonest citizen of the League — was trained from childhood to develop her physical strength and required to serve two years in the Guardians. Those who chose to make the military a career, as Soleyla had, spent six grueling years honing their fighting skills. More than once those skills had been all that stood between the League and destruction. The V'ranyii war, for example.

A single man with a knife? Soleyla grinned into the night.

She let herself go limp against him, so that his right arm was now supporting her not-inconsiderable weight. The knife wavered at her throat. Quick as lightning, she tilted her chin skyward and allowed herself to collapse. The sharp edge nicked the point of her chin, drawing blood, but she slid under it, twisting out of his grasp even as she drew her sword. She brought it around in a vicious swipe — and it clanged off steel.

"Did you really think I went unbladed, Guardian?"

The timbre of his deep, stern voice was doing odd things to her libido. He was no more than an outline against the star-strewn sky, as the moon casting its light over the plain below had not yet cleared the peak, but she could see he was as enormous as she'd guessed. He towered over her — but Soleyla had been trained since childhood to fight.

She feinted rapidly, and his sword was there to block hers. She attacked again — and again he caught her blade on his own, easily, almost contemptuously. Her blood rose, a combination of rage and unassuaged sexual need. Screaming her fury, she whirled her blade above her head and sprang at him. He leaped back, lithe as a cat, and came in low.

Now it was she who fended off his attack, her sword dancing lightly in her grip, while he rained blows like hammer strokes down upon her defense. Damnation, but he was quick! Spinning to the right, she barely avoided a vicious slash from his blade.

Who was he? And what was he doing on this empty planet?

Unless — and Soleyla paused, hearing her breath rasping in her throat — it wasn't so empty after all.

Kantou crouched by the fire, watching the flames dance mockingly before him. As the night cooled, he'd drawn on his shirt. He shivered now, lightly, and hugged himself.

What was *wrong* with him?

Oh, he knew, no one better, what had been done to him—he could still feel the cutting fire of the lash across his back, testament to the lady Rachel's fury. Yet he'd done everything she commanded, even servicing her other slaves under her watchful gaze. He'd done it without hesitation, and still she was not satisfied.

Just as her daughter, it seemed, was not satisfied to merely take him.

He remembered how Soleyla had held him with her will, ordering him to touch himself, making him tease himself to a point of bliss he'd never before known. Remembered, too, how she'd made even the burst of agony as he'd squeezed his balls at her command a part of that ecstasy, heightening it to delirium. Even now, as he hunkered by the fire, shivering, he could feel his cock hardening at the memory of her voice, whispering, commanding.

Squeeze it harder. But slowly. Slowly, my beauty.

He knew what she wanted. She wanted the absolute surrender he'd given her that day, before he'd known who she was. She wanted him to trust her, as he'd hungered to do, to put himself utterly, without reservation, in her hands. More, she wanted him to want that, too.

Don't you? Don't you, Kantou? a small voice inside him spoke, its tone as dry and mocking as the dancing flames.

He did. He wanted it so desperately it terrified him. He wanted to feel himself poised, as if on the edge of a knife, every nerve in his body thrumming with the pain of desire, racked by her demands to a fever pitch. God! He could not stop remembering the sound of her voice, controlling him, bending him to her wishes. He wanted to submit, gratefully, let her do to him whatever she desired, wanted her to fuck him in every way imaginable.

His lady. His . . . Love?

It was an archaic word, one he'd only read in some old book. He'd never heard it spoken. But it was the only word he could think of that seemed to fit this strange hunger, this need to lay himself, body and mind and soul, in her hands, to open himself utterly to her desires.

For the first time, he *wanted* to be a slave. Soleyla's slave. He wanted to cast aside his self-imposed isolation, to open himself, body and soul, to her. He wanted her to possess him, rule him . . .

Cherish him.

For all the fire in his loins at the memory of her voice, it was how she'd touched him afterward that undid him. Her hands gently stroking his hair, making him feel safe, protected. Valued.

You are more to me than just a pleasure slave.

Kantou shuddered, feeling a deep, burning shame. How could he have frozen like that? Withdrawn on the deepest level even as he offered her his body? A half-surrender, a token. And she'd known it. She'd turned away from him, furious. Had left him here in the darkness alone, exiled from her warmth, face to face with his fears — and desire.

Her mother had merely savaged his body. She could scar him, but never break him.

But Soleyla, he feared, could shatter his very soul.

A spasm of agony twisted his face. He shuddered in the night, trapped between his longing and his fear, furious with himself, terrified that she would reject him, take him back to Merkun . . .

No. She wouldn't do that. Amid all his uncertainties, the memory of her expression as she slapped the coins from Merkun's palm was the one solid point he could cling to. It was that gesture which had allowed him to find the courage to follow her out of Merkun's tent and into the sunlight — and to here. Antoros. Somehow he'd trusted that she wouldn't abandon him.

And this was how he repaid her, her kindness, her patience. A black welling of self-disgust drove him to his feet. Frightened but determined, he left the ring of firelight, following the clear scuffs of her boot-prints in the sandy dirt through the silent, moonlit night.

When he heard the faint, distant clash of steel on steel, somewhere over the crest of the ridge, he broke into a run.

CHAPTER SIX

Soleyla cursed, struggling to keep her blade up. It was unthinkable! This man, this *slave*, was actually beating her, driving her back against the cliff that towered above the small, flat outcropping they fought upon. She cast about desperately as she fended off his sword strokes but could find no avenue of retreat.

Even as she struggled, sweating, to block yet another heavy thrust of his sword, a grudging admiration for his skill crept through her. Then the moon cleared the tip of the peak and shone down onto the ridge, and Soleyla's breath caught in her throat.

Piercing eyes burned into her own, sending a bolt of white-hot lust straight through her loins. In the half-light she couldn't see their color, but they were clear and intense. Massive shoulders flexed easily, wielding a sword that looked well-used and sharp. He was older than she, with a heavy, grim set to his jaw that seemed almost feminine in its ferocity. It spoke of responsibilities, hard decisions—things that men never had to deal with. And he was most decidedly a man. His private parts were protected by a clout around his waist, but other than that he was utterly naked. His broad chest gleamed with sweat. The lower half of his belly was flat with muscle, dusted with dark hair . . .

Her eyes lingered a moment too long, and he used her inattention to slap her sword from her hand. *Damn!* Soleyla pressed herself flat against the rock, waiting stiffly for the killing blow.

It never came.

Instead, he tickled her throat with the point of his sword, using the flat of the blade to press her head back, exposing the nick she'd acquired when sliding free of his knife. He grunted, as if in satisfaction, and lowered his blade. He picked up her sword and flung it far into the darkness. She heard it rattle on stone and slide down the slope.

"Now," he said, "let's try this again. What are you doing here?"

Soleyla retreated into outraged formality. "I am a Guardian, dispatched by the League to secure this planet for future settlement."

"I knew that much. What are you doing *here*?"

She glared at him and stalked to a boulder. He watched her, eyes narrowed, ready to attack, but relaxed his stance when she sank down onto it, rubbing her sore shoulders. Three weeks spent hiking hadn't given her much chance to keep up her swordplay.

"Planting relay markers," she replied finally.

He squatted on his heels, resting his sword across his massive thighs. What a pleasure slave he would make! Wisely, Soleyla kept that opinion to herself.

"And what is a relay-marker?"

Soleyla stared. "It's a device . . . a transmitter. Who are you that you don't know that?"

He grinned, his eyes flashing with an intricate combination of irony and rue. "I didn't. Now I do. Who I am is unimportant."

Soleyla rather doubted that, but she didn't argue. Only the precariousness of her situation kept her from reveling in the sheer visual stimulation his body was providing. Or perhaps it was precisely that precariousness that was making her so keenly aware of his overwhelming maleness. She could smell the tangy, intoxicating scent of his sweat, could feel a surreptitious trickle of warmth run through her belly.

But then, she'd never been in a situation in the least like this. Pinned where she was by an armed male! It was ludicrous. But it was also, she admitted secretly, oddly arousing.

"The only problem, Guardian," he continued, "is that this planet you're preparing for settlement is already inhabited."

A vague memory stirred in her mind, a terse sentence in the information packet she'd been handed on arrival. Valda had hustled her out of the base camp before she'd had a chance to read half of it.

Evidence of native populace — suppress or exterminate. And here, she surmised, was the native populace. Nice of Valda to warn her.

But sharing that particular command with this enormous, armed man was hardly likely to increase her chances of survival. Then again, if he'd merely meant to kill her, she'd be dead already. The realization rankled. He'd beaten her, damn it! She, a decorated captain of the elite League Guardians!

And the sight of him, hunkered before her, was arousing other emotions besides her ire.

"That's what you are? A native?"

He inclined his head, assenting.

"I see. I wasn't aware." Which was only partially a lie. She'd forgotten all about that terse sentence in the briefing packet — until now.

"I didn't think you were, or you wouldn't have been climbing through the northern ranges alone. Your friends back there," he nodded eastward, toward the distant base camp, "wouldn't. They've learned better."

"Oh?" Soleyla sat forward. "Then it wasn't an oversight." With a sickening rush of rage, she knew Valda had purposely sent her out here without warning her.

At her mother's request. It had to be at her mother's request. Automatically, Soleyla's hand dropped to the hilt of her missing sword, and she cursed again.

The man followed her motion with a wry glance. "That wasn't intended for me, I'm thinking."

Soleyla shook her head, trying to clear it. Too much was happening, too quickly. She couldn't assimilate it.

"How many of you are there?"

He chuckled, long and low. "Come now, Guardian, you don't really expect me to give you that information."

No, she didn't. "At least give me your name."

"Give me yours."

Fair enough. "Soleyla."

He mouthed the syllables, his lips forming them silently as he stared down over the distant, moon-flooded plain. Soleyla shifted on the boulder, and she saw his muscles tense in readiness. She sat back, sighing. Escape would not be so easy as that.

His eyes flicked back to her, then returned to their surroundings. It was, she noticed belatedly, a breathtaking view. Moonlight spilled over the sharp, craggy mountains, giving them an eldritch beauty beneath the star-strewn sky. On the plain below, she noticed small points of light—campfires, likely. Maybe a village. She nodded toward it. "That's where you're from?"

He didn't reply. A fierce, passionate light glowed in his eyes, though, one she could hardly help understanding. "It's a beautiful planet," she said, meaning it.

"It's ours." His words were hard, uncompromising.

"They'll kill you for it."

His eyebrows shot up. "They?"

Soleyla felt her cheeks heat and was grateful for the darkness.

He studied her a moment, then turned away. "They already have," he said, his voice a whisper in the night. It sent shivers up her, raising the hairs on the back of her neck.

"Killed, and worse."

"What could be worse than killing?" The words were out of her mouth before she could stop them. She saw his face darken as he turned back toward her. His sword came up. Reflexively, she sprang up, backed away until she bumped against the cliff.

He approached, his head slung low, a murderous light in his eyes. "Tell me, Guardian, can you imagine what it's like to be taken against your will?"

He towered over her, glaring down, the flat of his sword pressed across her chest. She could feel the cold steel even through her shirt, and wondered if he was aware he'd pressed it against her nipples.

In the shadow of the cliff, his face was a cipher. She couldn't see his eyes as he hissed down at her. "They ambushed us at Tinker's Pass. Sixty of them, against a dozen of us. Eight fell under their swords—and those eight were the lucky ones."

"You escaped?" Soleyla was painfully aware of the rock at her back, the massive man before her. Heat radiated off his body, warm and distinct in the cool night. Stars sparkled over the line of his shoulder, high and far away. A wave of desire flowed through her at his nearness, and she closed her eyes to conceal it. To respond so to a man, a slave! She should be mortified at her body's response.

But she wasn't.

And he was no slave.

She felt, rather than saw, him nod. If he moved any closer, she'd be pressed against him, able to feel his massive chest against her cheek. But the sword still lay between them, the cold steel hardening her nipples.

"I escaped. And I saw what they did to my men."

Sixty Guardians of the rank and file, women who could never afford, as she had, to bring a pleasure slave with them.

Sixty Guardians and three men like this one? It took no great imagination for Soleyla to picture what had happened.

The man's grip tightened on her arm. "They used them unmercifully, until my men begged for death. Their screams haunt me, even now."

"I'm sorry," Soleyla whispered, realizing even as she said the words that they were true. What had been done to those men was as bad as what her mother had done to Kantou. Worse, even. They'd used the men's own bodies against them, forcing their captives to betray themselves on the most fundamental level.

Yes, she could imagine what that might be like.

"Sorry?" He spat into the dark. "I saw you! You and your pleasure-pet. I saw how you watched him, knowing you could have him whenever you wanted." His hand gripped her arm to the point of pain, and the flat of the sword dug into her breasts. "Why didn't you, Guardian? Why didn't you order him to his knees like the dog he is and make him service you?"

Soleyla shifted, trying to ease the pinch of his grip—and her thigh brushed against him. She froze in shock. This unknown barbarian was almost painfully erect! She could feel his cock straining at his breechclout.

"Answer me!" he commanded.

"You wouldn't believe me."

He glared down at her. "Answer."

The sword pressed harder and slid toward her throat.

"I wouldn't have him unwilling!" she shouted, suddenly furious, daring him to disbelieve her. All her patience, all her self-control, and this was where it had gotten her? How *dare* this man accuse her! She returned his glare, seeing moonlight line the curve of his heavy cheekbone. He was grinning, a hard, angry grin that made her blood run suddenly cold.

"No," he said, and Soleyla's throat went dry. "No more

unwilling than you'll be, I'm sure."

He ran his free hand up her, feeling the generous weight of her breasts. The sword tangled between them, and he threw it aside.

"There's only one blade I need with a woman," he murmured, and pulled her roughly against him.

What an odd joke. Soleyla had never heard a penis compared to a sword before. But as she felt his erection digging into the curve of her belly, she understood the comparison. It throbbed against her, eager to pierce her flesh. Arousal wrestled with her offended pride as he clamped his hands in her shirt and ripped it open. Her breasts tumbled out into the moonlight, their curves exposed fully to his view. She heard him groan with pleasure as his gaze locked firmly on her full, round orbs, and he closed his hands around them.

Involuntarily, she gasped, and he peered down at her.

"Do you like that, then?" He drew back, letting his fingers trail across her rock-hard nipples, then pinched them tightly between thumb and forefingers.

Soleyla's knees turned to water as waves of sharp anticipation spread from her aching nipples to her groin.

He shoved her back against the cliff, trapping both her wrists in one hand and holding them far above her head. He thrust the other into her pants, grazing it against her clit, then dipping lower to probe her wet sex.

"Ah, I see you do. Can barely wait for it, can you?" Cruelly, he closed his fingers on her clit—hard—and she bit off a shriek. She would not, she swore, give him the satisfaction of making her come.

He yanked his hand from her pants and ran it back over her breasts, squeezing first one, then the other, watching the nipples tighten further as he played with them roughly. His breath grew deeper, the muscles of his jaw relaxing in arousal. His eyes grew softer, darker, and he rocked his hips forward, pressing his cock against her. She could feel it, nudging against her clit, and closed her eyes in mingled shame and desire.

It wasn't supposed to be like this. She was not the one taken, but the taker! Yet every fiber in her yearned for his rough touch, ached to have him spread her wide and pierce her with his hardness, press her down into the rocky soil and savage her with his cock, his hands . . .

He yanked her downward, so quickly she hadn't time to even try to resist, and stretched her flat on the ground, her breasts pressing into his chest. He lowered his head, nipped sharply at them. The stimulus was almost more than she could bear, but Soleyla gritted her teeth and stiffened her spine against the sensations pulsing through her.

No man, she swore, would have the last word here.

Her arms lay flat at her sides, trapped under his heavy weight. With her fingertips she could feel the edge of a rock, sharp and hard and the size of her fist. She stroked one finger lovingly against it as he tugged at her belt, opening her pants and dragging them off. When he thrust his tongue between her damp, swollen lips, Soleyla forgot all about the rock.

He clamped his mouth around her pulsing clit, running his tongue over it again and again. He moaned at the taste of her—and Soleyla felt the vibration of that deep, humming sigh straight through her bones. Against her conscious will, her hands came up, burying themselves in his thick, sooty hair, drawing his mouth tighter against her as her hips pressed upward, urging him on.

He seized her hands, shoved them down at her sides. "Oh no, you League bitch. You don't rule here yet." Grabbing her thighs, he yanked them apart, exposing the warm, wet slit of her pussy to the cool night air. She gasped as a breeze played over her, stroking her sweaty body, licking at her nipples. Then it was gone, replaced by a hot, demanding cock pressing at her opening.

No. No, he would not have her so easily, no matter how she hungered for it. Soleyla tightened the muscles of her abdomen, tilting her hips back and making herself as inaccessible as possible. Still he pressed at her, his slick, velvety head bumping lightly at her clit. God, it felt so good!

"You want it like that, then?" he whispered, his voice rough with desire. "You want me to take you hard? For I *will* take you, Guardian."

His shaft slid back and forth over her swollen, aching nub. Soleyla tossed her head mindlessly, caught in the sensation between her legs. He lowered his head to one breast, sucking her nipple into his mouth. His tongue flicked against it, over and over, and to her horror, she heard herself panting, "Yes. Oh please, yes!"

She tilted her pelvis back further, making him fight to enter her. Her juices trickled freely between her thighs as he drove his shaft up into her. She felt his groan more than heard it, the vibration of his deep voice traveling straight through his chest and into hers. Wrapping her arms around him, she trailed her hands down his back, cupping his muscular ass and drawing him more tightly into her. He shoved himself up onto his arms and rocked, his pelvic bone pressed firmly against hers, his head thrown back as ecstasy took him, plunging into her faster and faster. She grabbed his ass-cheeks, spreading them slightly, hearing him gasp as the cool air tickled his balls.

Soleyla gripped him inside her, thrusting her hips upward, and worked one strong finger between his asscheeks and down to his hole, tickling the tight rim. He plunged into her, hard, his breath a ragged moan in the night.

"Ah, God, woman!"

Soleyla pressed against the muscle, feeling the resistance. No one had ever entered him before, she could tell. The thought sent a fresh wave of desire through her. But she had other reasons for making him want to lose all control.

Swiftly, she twisted under him, rolling him to one side. Before he could push her back down, she straddled him, seized his cock in one firm hand and shoved it back inside her. His neck extended as he tilted his head back, and his hands came up to cup her breasts.

"Oh God, yes," he breathed. "Ride me, woman."

She raised herself high above him, feeling his cock slide almost out of her, until the meaty lip of his cockhead dragged at her dripping folds. Then she plunged down, driving him into her, feeling the curls of his pubic hair tangle with her own as she rocked against him, completely impaled.

Again, she lifted slowly, teasing the full length of him. His head tossed with delirium. His hands pulled at her breasts. She could feel his shaft swelling, aching for release, and she slid herself down, gripping him inside her. His jaw gaped wide as he howled in pleasure, and Soleyla could feel his hot cum spurting, wave after wave of it, deep into her. His back arched as he pumped, drawing out every drop, and Soleyla smiled down at him as a satiated grin spread over his face.

That was when she hit him with the rock.

CHAPTER SEVEN

K antou scrambled to the crest of the rise and froze.
Moonlight bathed the outcropping, spilling down from
the heights of the peak onto the two bodies writhing before
his eyes. He watched Soleyla arch her hips up even as the
enormous man pressed downward, groaning with desire.
Dimly, he wondered where the man had come from, but the
question fled, unanswered, as Soleyla matched the stranger
stroke for stroke.

She rolled the man over, straddling him, her high firm
breasts gleaming in the moonlight. The man reached up to
cup them even as she rocked down on his shaft, sending him
deep into her. Kantou's own cock sprang fully erect. He
watched, gnawing at his lip, as the man squeezed and stroked
her beautiful breasts, throwing his head back in an excess of
lust.

Unable to watch any longer, Kantou retreated into the
darkness, pursued by the sounds of their coupling.

Blindly, he stumbled back down the ridge, feeling loose
stones and scree bounce away beneath his heedless descent.
His erection throbbed in his pants, but the strange burning in
his chest outweighed it. He felt tears straining at his throat,
and a black, bitter self-hatred welling up inside him.

How stupid could he be? She had wanted him—*him*—for
weeks, had waited patiently, showing a kindness no slave had
a right to expect. And he had flinched away from her, from
the touch that he secretly craved. It was no wonder, he
thought, his inner vision blacker than the night around him,

that she'd found relief with some other slave—wherever he had come from.

The tears spilled over, blurring his sight as he stumbled back to the campsite. The fire had burned low and dully he gathered wood, built it back up. At least she would have a light to guide her return.

If she returned. If she still wanted him.

Kantou remembered the man below her, gripped between her strong, slender thighs. He was massive, ruggedly handsome. Kantou bit his lip again, bitterly aware of his own slenderer build, his long, soft hair, his more delicate features. What had he to offer that could compete with that?

Woodenly, he moved about the circle of firelight, belatedly preparing the meal she'd commanded and setting the camp to rights. Then he heated water over the blazing fire and slowly, carefully, bathed himself. His cock throbbed as he washed it, but he ignored its demands. He was determined that everything would be perfect, waiting for her, when she returned.

If she returned.

A stab of anticipatory grief shot through him. Ruthlessly, he suppressed it.

If he'd lost her . . .

If he'd lost her, what was left for him?

But if he hadn't, he swore to himself, he would do all in his power to win her attentions back.

Naked, dripping, fully erect, he knelt in the firelight, facing the path she was most likely to come. He bent his head and waited.

Soleyla checked the man's pulse. He was still breathing. The cut on his head trickled blood, but not much. She stared down at him, feeling his cock still inside her, soft now. What was she to do with him?

She moved, and a painful throb of unreleased tension shot through her pussy as she felt him slide out. Well, she had won, for all the good it had done her. She hadn't let him make her come. Now she was paying the price of her victory, damn him!

Roughly, she used her sword-belt to bind his wrists. He was too huge to move, so she left him lying there as she picked up his sword and threw it, whistling, over the edge of the outcropping. It spun through the air and disappeared into the darkness. Far below, she heard a soft clang and nodded, satisfied.

Pulling her pants back on and tugging her clothes into some semblance of order, she started down the slope, pausing only to retrieve her own sword from where he'd tossed it. The cloth of her pants rubbed irritatingly against her swollen mons, so that the hike down merely exacerbated her frustration rather than dispelling it as she'd hoped.

Her rage, too, had not diminished. For all that she had craved the encounter, nevertheless it rankled that he'd beaten her. And, she admitted, he would have taken her, would have used her as a woman uses a pleasure slave, if she hadn't been willing. She had said 'yes,' but 'no' would have been meaningless. It would not have stopped him.

The admission sickened her, made her skin crawl. Outrage welled through her, and she felt a sudden desire to do the same to him, have him at her mercy, unwilling, screaming in pain. Rage throbbed in her temples. That someone could do that to *her*, Soleyla Devarian, daughter of —

Soleyla froze.

Daughter of Rachel Devarian, Regent of Argulus.

Rachel Devarian, who would not hesitate to use a man far worse than this man had used her daughter. Rachel Devarian, whom Soleyla could so easily picture among those sixty

Guardians, raping a man until he begged to die.

Rachel Devarian, senior Senator of the Nine-Star League. The woman who, Soleyla had sworn, she was nothing like.

Soleyla's hands flew to her mouth. Then she vomited into a clump of bushes.

It was much, much later when she stumbled into the camp, her sword dangling from her exhausted grip. She paid no attention to Kantou as she staggered past him to her bedroll, aching in every fiber of her body.

Soleyla lay on her back, her muscles slack and unresponsive. But her mind was whirling too fast for sleep. Who, she wondered, was she? Daughter of a regent who'd tried to have her killed, Guardian of a League which had sent her, and others, to conquer a planet.

Evidence of native populace – suppress or exterminate. Was *that* what she'd fought for, what she'd sworn to uphold?

They used them unmercifully, until my men begged for death.

Because they *were* men. And men were slaves, nothing more. To be used for their bodies until they died.

That was how it was. That was how it was supposed to be. Wasn't it?

Soleyla's head ached.

She heard a harsh noise and lifted her head, feeling a fresh throb at her temples as she did so. Squinting her eyes against the pain, she made out Kantou, squatting near the fire where he'd been when she returned. He was, she realized belatedly, naked. And he was crying.

"Kantou."

He raised his head. Tears coated his cheeks. A poignant vulnerability shone in his eyes.

"Kantou, what . . ."

She dropped her head back, too tired even for that exertion, and gestured weakly. Immediately, he was beside her, wiping his cheeks with the back of his hand.

"My lady?"

She shook her head wearily. "No. Just Soleyla." He stared at her, uncomprehending. She sighed and reached out her hand. He took it, almost reverently, stroked his long, clever fingers along it. His touch was so soothing. She felt him turn her hand over and kiss the palm lightly. He moved down to her feet, gently removing her boots, pulled one foot onto his lap and began rubbing it.

"Mmm," she murmured, and relaxed into his touch, floating on the waves of sensation as he pressed his thumbs into her arch, kneading away the tight bands of tension.

I shouldn't let him do this, she thought, half-asleep. It was wrong, something about the very fabric of their society was very, very wrong. But she was so tired, she couldn't puzzle it out and his hands felt so good . . .

Distantly, she felt him tugging off her pants, digging his fingers into her sore calves. Then her thighs. A warm, delicious languorousness spread through her belly, making her vaguely horny. A wet, gentle pressure built in her groin as his tongue lapped softly against her exposed clit . . .

Soleyla sat up abruptly. "Kantou, no!"

He cowered back, quivering. Soleyla cursed again, long and loud. She was so fucking tired, but sleep had fled, leaving her nerves jangling, stretched to a breaking point. She stared down at Kantou, breathing heavily, willing her rage back.

Then she squatted by him, gently lifted his chin so his eyes gazed into hers. She smiled softly. "Kantou, no. You don't need to do that."

"But, my lady, you said —"

"I know what I said." *Where, when, and as I like.* Her arrogant words rang in her memory, and Soleyla scowled blackly. Then quickly wiped the expression away as she saw him flinch back. "I know what I said, Kantou, but that's not what I want."

Tears welled up in his eyes. Damn it all! What had she said to upset him now? "What is it?"

He glanced away. His voice was a whisper, so soft she had to bend close to hear it. "I know, my lady."

"Know what?"

"That you don't want me anymore." His voice ached with grief.

Soleyla stared at him, dumbfounded. What? She didn't want him? Horrified, she felt a giggle rising through her, surprised out of her by exhaustion and the absurdity of the situation.

And why should he care, anyway? He was a slave, constrained to obey her, whether he wanted to or not. She'd assumed it would be a relief to be freed of that.

He turned his face toward her, his cheeks damp with tears. "It's all right, my lady. I know you don't want me. I saw you, with him, before — "

Soleyla's eyes widened. "You followed me?"

He nodded.

"Why?"

"Because," he stammered, "because I denied you. I offered my body, but my heart . . . Oh, my lady, I was so afraid. And now that I've lost you . . ."

"Lost me?" Shock made her tone sharp, and he cringed. "Kantou! You're a slave! Why should you care if I want you or not?"

"I don't know, I don't know," he sobbed, wrapping his arms around himself and rocking like a child. Moved by his distress, Soleyla reached out and drew him against her. He cowered against her breast, shuddering, and she held him, murmuring sounds that were barely words, low and soothing, as she stroked his hair.

Eventually his shudders eased, and Soleyla lifted her head. Above the mountains, the sky had faded to a soft, hazy purple as dawn drew near. What a strange, unexpected night it had been. She looked down at Kantou, sure he was asleep, and was surprised to find his gray eyes open, staring up at her.

"I don't know," he repeated in a whisper. "All I know is I can't live without you."

She felt her throat tighten at the raw need in those words, a need that ran deeper than anything she'd ever imagined. Something in her breast ached, almost like the grief she'd felt at the loss of Danel. Losing him had felt like losing a part of herself.

How had Kantou come to feel such need for her?

The question was unimportant. What was important was that he was hers, beyond any binding of law or purchase. He was hers because she'd made him so, because she'd demanded no less than the full gift of his soul.

Now she had it — and it humbled her.

She stroked his long hair back from that high, smooth forehead, studying the beautiful, chiseled planes of his face.

At her touch, his eyes closed in an ecstasy which had nothing to do with lust. His face turned toward her, his cheek grazing her breast and softly, delicately, he nuzzled at its fullness. His lips closed around her nipple, pulling it into his mouth and Soleyla watched, feeling a gentle heat build through her as he suckled greedily, his jaw working, his head resting against her arm. He glanced up at her once, as if for reassurance, and she closed her eyes for a moment, giving herself over to the sensation. His hand came up, cupped her other breast, and she arched her back, pressing herself into his touch.

Emboldened, he squeezed harder, drawing his fingers across the silken curve to her other nipple, teasing it between his fingers, flicking them across its nubbly surface, sending small electric shocks coursing through her. Mindlessly, she tilted her head back, let him lower her down onto her mat as his head moved, his tongue caressing her belly, her thighs . . .

Like a snake it darted between her legs, and she felt him lapping her, tasting her juices — and, she remembered suddenly, the stranger's juices as well. She started to sit up and was amazed when he pushed her gently back.

"No," he breathed, his lips tickling her lightly. "Let me eat him out of you, my lady. Please."

"Are you sure this is what you want, Kantou?" She felt his rough nod, then was aware of nothing but his tongue darting into her fiercely, lapping all traces of the other man's cum from her. She moaned as he spread her legs further, sent his tongue thrusting deeper, and then slid it lower until it prodded at the small, tight hole she'd allowed no one to touch. Soleyla gasped at the sensation and raised her hips.

Kantou cupped his hands under them, lifting her to him, and drove his tongue against her asshole again and again. A strange, yearning ache built up inside her, and she shoved herself against him, wanting him to pierce her, to force his tongue past that tight ring of muscle . . . When she felt his finger moving beside his tongue she moaned like a wild animal.

Gently, slowly, he worked his finger inside her, sliding his tongue constantly around her stretched skin. Lubricated with his spit, his finger slid easily, deeper and deeper. She could feel it pressing nerves she'd never been aware of, building the ache inside her to a hot, ravenous hunger. Her hips moved of their own accord, urging him on, and he slicked his finger back and forth, stretching the muscle, waiting till it relaxed, opening fully to him.

"Oh, more," she gasped, and squirmed with pleasure as she felt a second finger join the first, spreading her wider. It stung, but only briefly, and then his fingers were pumping deliriously as his tongue danced over her throbbing clit.

"God," she breathed, rocked by the sensation. She could come right now, if she let herself. But she didn't want to. She wanted to tease this out, stretch him to the very limits of his endurance, dominate his every nerve and fiber—for both their sakes.

Gently, she pulled herself away, and he slid his fingers out of her slowly and sat back, kneeling between her thighs. She looked up, reveling in the sight of him, poised beneath the lightening sky, his enormous cock hard and jutting in the soft morning air. She could barely wait to have that massive, throbbing shaft inside her. She wanted him to fuck her until there was nothing in the galaxy but the pounding of his cock inside her. But first . . .

First she would fuck *him*.

Soleyla smiled. "All right," she said. "You got my attention."

The smile that spread over his features at her words made her heart clench again in a sharp, almost painful wave of emotion. *Mine*, she thought fiercely with a deep, possessive pride as she watched her beautiful, needy, loving Kantou.

Mine.

CHAPTER EIGHT

The emotion that suffused him was almost religious in its intensity. She wanted him. Kantou sighed to himself. She *wanted* him.

The desire that glowed in her eyes ignited his own. She was so stunning, stretched out before him, her hair tousled in the soft morning light. He could still taste the salty-sweet tang of her. He licked his lips, savoring every last trace. The aftertaste of semen only heightened her own flavor. He felt his cock pulsing between his legs but made no move to touch it. Not until she told him to.

She wanted *him*.

That realization alone made his balls ache with pleasure. He could come, he thought, for hours, just so she could watch. He would do anything for her.

Anything, and everything. His cock twitched at the idea.

She watched it, an amused smile playing about her lips. Her eyes sparkled speculatively, and he felt his breath go short in anticipation.

"Turn around," she said, and his throat clenched at her low, commanding murmur, like the purr of a tiger. "Turn around, Kantou, and kneel before me."

He did, feeling the skin on his back twitch, waiting for her touch. She trailed her fingers slowly down his spine, curving her hands over the cheeks of his ass. He shivered and felt his sphincter throb hopefully.

"Do you like that, Kantou?"

"Oh yes, my lady."

Laying her palm flat between his shoulder blades, she pushed him forward onto all fours, then down, so that his chest pressed the ground. Shoving her knee between his thighs, she forced his legs further apart. He felt the tendons running up the inside of his thighs stretch, and pictured himself as he must appear to her—legs spread, ass pointed at the sky, wide open and inviting. He whimpered lightly, feeling his cock press against his belly.

She started with his thighs, running her hands up the delicate inner skin with a feathery touch, then down again. Over and over until he quivered and shook, his breath hissing through his teeth in short, eager gasps. Then she moved to his balls, batting them playfully like a kitten, cupping their weight in her strong, limber fingers. They were so tight, so full of cum they dragged at his cock, tugging it lightly each time she squeezed them.

Surreptitiously, he slid his hands to his nipples, pinched them lightly, then twisted them as she slid her hands up his ass, spreading it wider, and pressed her mons hard against his hole. Kantou arched his back, rubbing himself against her, aching to be taken, to be split apart under her loving touch. He would be her wanton, her slave, her toy to break and trample—anything she wanted. However she used him was pleasure to him.

"Kantou?" she breathed, her voice deep and smoky.

"Yes, my lady."

"What do you want, Kantou?"

"Whatever will please you."

"No!" A sharp smack, and his ass stung beneath her slap. His skin twitched, burning with sensation, and he felt his cock jerk, spilling the first beads of cum. He felt them drip from the head to fall into the dirt. He moaned, pistoning his ass higher.

"Try again. What do you want, Kantou?" Her voice was low, erotically dangerous. Kantou swallowed in a very dry throat.

"I want you to fuck me," he whispered into the dirt, shivering as she spanked him again.

"What was that? I can't hear you."

"I want you to fuck me, my lady."

"Say my name," she hissed.

His heart bucked, thundering in his ears, driving a fresh wave of blood through his body. His cock swelled still further, brushing his navel. "Soleyla."

How sweet her name felt on his tongue. As smooth and delicious as her huge, stunning breasts. "Soleyla," he whispered again, tasting the sounds, rolling them between his full, throbbing lips.

"Tell me again."

"Fuck me, Soleyla. I want you to fuck me."

"More," she commanded tersely, and Kantou felt something inside him let go with a snap. He rubbed his cheek against the dirt, murmuring deliriously, "I want you to fuck my ass. Split me open. Make me hurt, make me scream. Oh please, please, Soleyla!"

"Very touching, to be sure," said a deep, mocking voice, and Kantou felt his lady's hands freeze on his ass. "But I'm afraid I really don't see how she can."

Kantou looked up to see the stranger sitting on a rock, watching them with a derisive smile. A shadow flickered off to the right.

Kantou scrambled to his feet as another man—blond, this one, but as large as the first—stepped into the clearing. Three more followed. Soleyla sprang up and swept up her sword, placing herself between Kantou and their adversaries. The dark-haired one laughed at that and nodded to the others.

Soleyla swung wildly as they rushed her, but there were too many. They pinioned her sword arm, wrenched away the blade, and grabbed her. Desperately, Kantou sprang at them, and one man thrust him, sprawling, in the dirt.

"Kantou!" Soleyla screamed, and he struggled to reach her as they dragged her away. Then a heavy boot connected with his forehead, and he knew no more.

He awoke hours later, struggling. His hands were bound behind his back. Harsh fibers gritted under his cheek. He was lying on a rug, on the floor of a tent. Slowly, his eyes focused.

The tent was large, dim, with only a trickle of sunlight around the edges of the flap. There was a bed made of heaped skins on one side, a table, two low carved chairs. Someone sat in one of them.

Kantou sat up carefully, his head pounding with agony. The shape spoke, and he recognized that same deep, mocking voice.

"There's water, if you want it." The man nodded at a low table. Awkwardly, Kantou crawled to it, lowered his face to the shallow basin and gulped greedily.

"Where is she?" he demanded as soon as he raised his head.

The man quirked a dark, heavy eyebrow. He was dressed, Kantou saw, in nothing but a clout and some sort of fur thrown over his huge, broad shoulders. Kantou raged inwardly against the man's sheer mass. How could he fight a giant like that?

He crouched, glaring, demanded again, "Where is she?" The man merely watched him.

Anger flared through Kantou, and he lunged at the man. Contemptuously, the stranger stuck out a foot, tumbling him back to the rug.

"Don't worry, little slave. Your mistress is perfectly safe — and more comfortable, I'm certain, than how she left me."

Kantou's gaze flicked to the man's wrists, noted the red, angry welts there. "Take me to her," he demanded.

His opponent chuckled. "Spoken almost like a man, little slave. What's your name?"

Kantou clenched his jaw. The man smiled, flashing his teeth. They were strong and white, large like all the rest of him. Kantou felt despair trickling into his belly.

"I already know hers, if that helps free your tongue." Kantou remained mute.

The man shrugged. "Suit yourself." He lounged back in his seat as a woman — Kantou stared — entered quietly, set a tray with meat and bread and a small pitcher of oil on the table, and withdrew.

Like a servant, Kantou thought. *Like a slave.* "What have you done with her?" he demanded.

"Ah, the slave speaks."

He drew himself up — as well as he could with his bonds. "My name is Kantou."

The man smiled. "But still a slave, for all that. I am Rolen, since you refuse to ask."

Kantou watched him stonily. "I am Soleyla's, yes, if that's what you mean."

The man — Rolen — stared. "Are you so broken that you're proud of that?"

Proud? It was something Kantou had never considered. But yes, remembering the light in his lady's eyes, the possessive hunger in them. Yes, he was proud of it.

But how could he explain that to this huge, caustic man?

"You wouldn't understand."

"Then explain it."

"I can't."

Rolen studied him narrowly. He seemed to Kantou almost feminine in his fierceness. Those sharp blue eyes shone with piercing intelligence. Kantou held himself stiff under that scrutiny, refusing to move. Outside he could hear voices in the distance, the sound of people walking past the tent.

Rolen watched him, puzzled. How could a man bend himself to a woman so? He remembered the sight of this slave, this Kantou, on his knees, his ass displayed like a wanton's, begging her to fuck him. Could the slave really be as meek as he seemed?

No. There was nothing meek about Kantou now. There was a fire in him, clear to anyone with eyes to see. And he was no weakling, Rolen could see that. Strong as the woman was, he could likely take her — no, he corrected himself, remembering her swordplay. The bitch knew how to fight. And he was quite certain this overhung lapdog — bred for that enormous cock, most likely — couldn't.

Still, he could hardly love the feel of his face in the dirt, eating dust at her command. Forced to spread himself wide for her, making him beg her for the most demeaning act a man could suffer . . . Rolen's balls still tingled at the memory of the sight.

How could any living man not long to be free?

Yet here was Kantou, bristling before him, clothed in nothing but a dignity beyond Rolen's comprehension. Kantou with his luminous gray eyes and terrible scars on his back. Rolen had almost spitted the woman where she lay trussed on the ground when he first saw those scars.

Yet Kantou's first question had been to ask where she was.

She was, in fact, very close by, though Soleyla had no way of knowing that. She held her eyes closed to a slit, feigning sleep as the tent-flap opened and a small, roughly garbed woman entered. But the smell of food rising from the tray the woman carried roused Soleyla's hunger, and her stomach growled, betraying her.

"Ah, you're awake, right enough. No use pretending."

Discarding the deception, Soleyla pulled herself into a sitting position. The woman squatted before her, dressed in dun-colored skirts. She herself was naked—and trussed, hand and foot.

The woman held out food for her and she bent to it hungrily. "There you go. Slowly. You've slept the day through."

Soleyla could feel the woman studying her curiously, dwelling on the broad, heavy muscles of her shoulders, the old scar from a training fight across her upper thigh. But she was a woman, like Soleyla. Surely she would help her.

"Release me," she whispered, bending close.

"Ah." The woman chuckled. "It'd be more than I'm good for, setting you free. Rolen'd have no end of grief to give me."

"Rolen?" That was his name, then, the man who'd abducted her. "Is he your—I mean . . ." She stopped, confused. What sort of relations did men and women have on this planet? No slaves, no owners. She couldn't picture it.

But the woman seized her meaning anyway and laughed merrily. "Rolen? No. It'd take more than I'm up for to be *his* woman. I'm Jerril's."

"His slave, you mean?"

"Heavens, no." The woman looked shocked.

"But . . . Who gives the orders? Who decides what is to be done?"

"Ah," the woman nodded. "As far as that, it's Rolen. He leads us now, since his father was slain."

A *man*? She remembered the set of his jaw, the sense of responsibility no man should have to carry. Remembered, too, the anguished catch in his voice as he'd spoken of his men.

"What does he want of me?"

The woman shook her head. "Information, likely. He'll not harm you, if that's what you're worried about."

She wasn't, particularly. But she was still a captive. And

more than that . . ."Where's Kantou?"

"The one they brought with you?"

Soleyla nodded, her jaw tightening. If they'd dared to hurt him . . .

"With Rolen. He's fine. In more than one sense, I must say." The woman gave her a broad, lascivious grin. "I'm Maris," she added.

"Soleyla." Instinctively, she liked this woman, strange as Maris seemed to her. She was so playful, her smile so light-hearted. She seemed almost childlike to Soleyla, for all she must be a good eight years older, free of the responsibilities that every woman of the League carried as her natural burden.

But whether she liked Maris or not, Soleyla was bound, and needed to be free. She leaned forward, as if requesting more food. When Maris bent down to her, Soleyla slammed her head against the other woman's. Maris collapsed with a grunt.

Quickly, Soleyla rolled, bringing her hands into contact with Maris's belt knife. Carefully, she slit her bonds and stood, working blood back into her cramped feet. She was naked, but there was no help for that. She didn't dare pause to strip Maris of her clothing—which would be an ill fit anyway, she mused, regarding the smaller woman.

It didn't matter. She had to find Kantou.

Her sword was leaning in a corner. She seized it up, peered out the tent-flap, pleased that it was already nearly full dark. Sliding out of the tent, she slipped silently around the corner, flitting through the spaces between the tents.

Rolen sat back, puzzled. He helped himself from the tray as he studied Kantou. He was handsome, Rolen had to admit, his classic profile and lean, chiseled body almost breathtaking in their beauty. There was a will here, a strong one. It showed in the way the smaller man held himself stiffly, refusing to give any sign of the hunger he must feel.

Will, and good self-control.

"I've misjudged you, slave. You're more of a man than I thought."

Kantou bowed his head, as if acknowledging his tacit apology. Like an equal. *Is that it?* Rolen wondered. *Is he so conditioned that all men – even I – are slaves in his eyes, no better than him?*

The question roused his ire. "So tell me, Kantou. What is there to be proud of in being beaten by a woman?"

Kantou's eyes darkened. "She would not do that."

"She has. I saw the scars on your back."

Kantou shook his head in absolute denial. "That was not her."

"But it could have been, slave."

"No."

"It could have been."

"No."

Rolen snorted contemptuously. "Come, little slave." He leaned forward and slit Kantou's bindings. "Eat."

Kantou ate ravenously. Rolen watched him, noting the soft, full lips, the long, gleaming hair. Well, that was what he was bred for, after all. "Doesn't it bother you to know that she could?"

Kantou paused, his gray eyes distant, thinking. Then he nodded. "Yes. I see what you're saying."

"Then why not join us, Kantou? Join us, and be a free man?"

There was no pause at all before Kantou shook his head. Rolen sat back, nonplussed. "Do you love being a slave?"

"*Her* slave, yes." He looked up, his eyes bright and quick, studying Rolen. "What do you want of her?"

Rolen chuckled, masking his unease. Sharp, this one. And

utterly incomprehensible. "What makes you think I want anything of her?"

"You haven't killed us."

"True." Rolen shrugged it off and reached for a wine-flask. But Kantou's next question made him freeze.

"Why me, then? You want *something* of her. Badly, I'd say. So why waste your time talking to me?"

Rolen uncorked the flask and took a long draught before answering. "To understand her. Her, you, this whole damned League that's killing my people."

Kantou shook his head. "You can't."

"Why?"

"Because you look at me and see only the scars."

Rolen sat, struck mute by his words. Kantou continued. "You cannot understand because to you I'm an abomination. A man who submits himself to a woman's will. In your world, the man commands, the woman obeys."

"That's different."

"Does no man here ever beat his woman?"

"No! I . . . Sometimes," Rolen admitted grudgingly. "But the woman can leave."

"And go where? With another man? One who might beat her, as well?"

Furious, Rolen sprang up, his knife in his hands. He towered over Kantou, still kneeling on the floor. "You know nothing of us, slave! How *dare* you pass judgment?"

"Perhaps because you have passed judgment on him."

Rolen spun to see Soleyla standing before him, naked, legs braced, sword held at the ready. *Gods*, he thought, *what a woman!* She was like the warrior princesses legends spoke of. Legends, he realized suddenly, that were probably born of those same Guardians that his most ancient ancestors had fled from to Antoros, to escape their cruelty.

Rolen grabbed Kantou, dragged him to his feet, and

pressed the knife against the smaller man's throat. "Drop it, Guardian. Or your pleasure-pet dies."

CHAPTER NINE

Soleyla glanced at Kantou. His eyes were wide, but not panicked. He seemed as yet unharmed. She studied the stern man holding him, then dropped her sword.

"Good. Have a seat."

She did, glaring as he tied her hands behind the rough-carved chair.

"I'm glad you could join us, Guardian. We've been having a most interesting discussion." He motioned harshly at Kantou, indicating he should seat himself on the floor. Kantou purposefully strode to Soleyla and sat at her feet.

"Ever the lapdog," Rolen sneered. He seated himself and poured some wine.

He was every bit as massive as Soleyla remembered. Short, thick hair as black as ravens' wings fell over eyes that were a stern, clear blue. His jaw and cheekbones looked carved of granite. Soleyla felt a tingle that wasn't exactly made of fear. "What do you want?"

"I'm afraid we didn't have a chance to finish our conversation last night."

She glared. "If that's what you want to call it."

He laughed at that, throwing back his heavy head. The cords of his thick neck stood out clearly.

"That wasn't what I meant, though as I recall that ended a bit abruptly, too." He raised one hand to the back of his head, feeling the lump she'd left there. "But when I woke, I remembered something you said. Something that puzzled me, Soleyla."

Kantou stiffened at the sound of his voice speaking her name. The other man's piercing blue eyes flicked to him, noting his reaction, then moved back to Soleyla. "Your pet there doesn't like that, I think. Me knowing your name."

"I'm not sure I like it either." The fact was that his voice, pronouncing her name in his deep, oddly accented tones, was having precisely the effect on her it'd had the night before. Bound, at his mercy, she felt something more than a tingle. *Damn him!* "Get to it, Rolen. What did I say?"

He tilted his head back, narrowing his eyes, watching her keenly from under those dark brows. "You said 'they,' Guardian."

She froze, eyeing him warily. Rolen smiled to himself. He'd touched a sore spot there, he was certain. She sat across from him, bristling, gloriously naked — and utterly unafraid.

In fact, it occurred to him, the only time he'd seen her show the slightest trace of fear was when Kantou had been threatened. Rolen frowned. It was hardly what he'd expected, no matter how pretty the play toy.

He shook away that puzzle. Whatever they did between themselves didn't concern him. His people, and their survival, did.

"You said, '*They* will kill you for it.' Not 'we.' I want to know why."

"You kidnapped us just to ask me that question?"

He nodded.

"Why?"

He felt his jaw clench, his massive shoulders tightening. "Because you were right. They *will* kill us for this planet. And I've no way to stop them." Trying to keep the desperation he felt from his voice, he leaned forward. "I want your help, Guardian Soleyla."

"You chose an odd way to get it." Soleyla smiled thinly. She glanced down at Kantou, curled at her feet. "Did he harm you?"

Kantou shook his head.

"I had no choice," Rolen replied. "Fully a third of my people have been killed by your advance team. I would ask your forgiveness, but under the circumstances, I can't."

Soleyla nodded. "But why not simply approach me?"

"And get myself skewered? I think not."

"If I'd wanted to kill you, I'd have done it last night."

Rolen grinned ruefully. "You had me off my guard, alright." That was putting it mildly. She'd made him come like an overeager boy. He felt his cock twitch below the table and.

It was damnably hard to concentrate with her sitting there naked—and tied, too, he reminded himself, feeling a quick heat in his loins. The bonds pulled her arms back behind her, forcing her breasts up and out in a way that was highly distracting. Firmly, he looked away. "I cannot expose my people to unnecessary risk. Surely you can understand that."

"If you wish me to help you, you might start by trusting me," she shot back.

A hard woman, indeed. He switched tactics. "Who put those scars on your pretty boy's back? Kantou tells me it wasn't you."

She stiffened. "No. It was my mother."

"I see."

"I doubt it," she replied. Then sighed. "May I have some wine?"

He nodded, and Kantou reached for the flask, pouring her a glass. Rolen was bemused by the way he held it, eyes cast down, everything about him now radiating a meek submissiveness. Was this the same man who had defied him, only minutes ago in this very tent? It hardly seemed possible.

There was something sensual about the way he knelt, passive, waiting . . . And the way she accepted his attentions. Barely acknowledging his presence. And yet . . .

And yet she'd surrendered herself at the first hint of risk to her slave. Rolen shook his head, confused.

She sat back, and Kantou removed the cup from her lips. A droplet of wine clung to them, red and moist, as she closed her eyes. Her face was so still for a moment Rolen thought she was falling asleep on him.

Then, eyes still closed, she spoke, her words clipped, distant. "My mother is the regent of Argulus IV. The oldest planet of the League, and the most powerful. When I was sixteen, she bought me my first pleasure slave, Danel. Then, six years later, she took him away."

"Why?" Rolen was transfixed by the unspoken grief in her voice. Slave or no, she'd cared for this Danel deeply.

Soleyla opened her eyes, and immediately Rolen regretted the question. Something looked out of those eyes, something dangerous and desperately bleak. A look that reminded him of his own feelings, the night he'd lain in the darkness and listened to the tortured pleas of his men. He was relieved when she didn't answer.

Rolen cleared his throat and asked gently, "What happened to him?"

"I don't know." Her expression was distant, flat — it'd be so easy to mistake it for indifference, if he hadn't heard the naked pain in her voice.

She looked straight at him and asked, "Tell me, Rolen, what right did she have to do that?"

He cleared his throat, roughly. "He was a slave."

Her eyes closed again. Strangely, Rolen felt an urge to reach out to her, take her in his arms. This woman who spoke so easily of owning a man. No, he realized. Not easily at all. There were layers of pain here he couldn't begin to unravel.

"You don't understand me, I think." She gazed at him now, her eyes dark with an emotion he could not read. "Nor Kantou."

"I must confess, my lady, his attitude puzzles me." He looked at the man, larger and stronger than the woman he served, sitting so meekly at her feet.

"You shall," she said, then breathed one more word. "Kantou."

Kantou looked up. He'd followed the conversation closer than Rolen would ever have guessed, hearing nuances this Antorean could not begin to understand. And what he heard in that one word, his name, was that Soleyla had set him free.

He was a slave no longer.

He stood, his eyes on Rolen who was watching them closely, uncomprehending, as he bent to Soleyla and for the first time kissed her softly on the lips.

"Thank you, my lady," he murmured. Then he turned back to Rolen. "You know what she's done, of course."

"I can't say that I do."

"She's released me. Could you not hear it?"

Rolen shook his head and glanced at Soleyla, his brow knotted uncertainly. She stared back at him, silent.

"Would you like to see, Rolen, how I use my freedom?"

Rolen's piercing eyes darted back and forth between the two of them. "Is this a joke?"

"No joke," Kantou assured him, and picked up the knife from the table.

Rolen stiffened, but Kantou turned away from him to cut the ropes around Soleyla's wrists. Then he sank back down by her feet and laid his head in her lap.

Soleyla dropped a hand to his head, running her fingers gently through his hair, and looked challengingly at Rolen.

"I don't believe it," he said.

"No," said Soleyla, "you don't *understand* it." Kantou lifted his head, and she smiled down at him gently. "If he is no slave, Rolen, then no one can ever take him from me." She raised her eyes. "I will help you, Rolen. But then you will help *me."*

"Help you with what?" Rolen's attention lingered on the motions of her hand, running over and through Kantou's long, ash-brown hair.

Soleyla smiled. "You will help me overthrow the Nine-Star League."

Chapter Ten

"**W**hat?" Rolen sprang to his feet. "Woman, are you mad?"

"Sit down," she ordered. It was a voice that had commanded more than just slaves. It had commanded Guardians in battle. Rolen hesitated, then drew his chair back to the table.

"Thank you. Now . . ." She glanced down at Kantou. He looked back at her, his eyes luminous, waiting. "It isn't good to ally yourself with people you despise, Rolen."

"I don't—" he began.

She cut off his words with a motion. "Of course you do. Because you do not understand. Now, Rolen, you will."

Soleyla couldn't deny the erotic attraction of what she was about to do. But it wasn't lust that moved her to it—it was necessity.

He was a slave.

When Rolen had spoken those words, so much had crystallized for her. Because Danel was a slave, her mother had had the right, the authority, to take him away. Because Kantou was a slave, her mother could beat him.

And the Nine-Star League gave her that right.

Soleyla looked at Kantou. *No one* had the right to take him away. He had given himself to her, utterly. Forever. And if something threatened that? Then that something must go.

And for that, she needed Rolen, needed his strength, and the strength of every man he commanded. But how could he fight for something he couldn't understand?

Freedom he understood — the freedom to dominate, to decide, to conquer. It was that drive that had, if old tales were true, almost destroyed humanity before it ever reached the stars. That will to dominate was, in men, so strong and so innate that the wars they had started had almost wiped out the species. It was for that reason women had first seized power.

Now the pendulum had swung too far. It was time to correct it. But there was more than one kind of freedom that needed protection. There was also the freedom to submit. To obey. To serve. And there was a beauty and a strength in it that this man would never see.

Not unless he was shown.

Kantou knelt silently at her feet. His incredible cock jutted, purple and erect, from between his thighs. A stab of hunger flared through Soleyla, along with a momentary pang of regret. She wanted him so badly, wanted that massive cock inside her, wanted to seal the binding between them with that most intimate of sharing.

But there were more important things at stake in this room than her desires. "Kantou," she breathed again.

Those marvelous gray eyes, so quick, so penetrating, rose to her face, studying her. She thought she saw a brief flash of regret as he realized what she needed of him. Then he bowed his head.

"What is my lady's will?"

Soleyla fixed her gaze on Rolen, pinning him with her eyes as she slid her hands under her breasts, cupping them. She saw his eyes widen, the pupils dilating.

"Lick them, Kantou. Now."

Rolen stared as Kantou leaned forward, carefully touching Soleyla with nothing but his tongue. He could see the younger man's cock, larger than Rolen's own, fully erect. It pulsed with arousal, and yet Kantou never touched it, never so much as brushed it against her thigh as his tongue worked steadily over one breast, then the other. Rolen felt his breath grow short as Kantou's deft tongue flicked at her nipples, making the points rise, hard and pink.

God! How did he do it? If it were him, Rolen admitted, he would already have dragged her from her chair and thrown her to the ground, spreading her thighs . . .

As if reading his thoughts, Soleyla smiled languorously, clearly enjoying Kantou's attentions. She glanced at Rolen's hand which had, without him being aware of it, been sneaking toward his crotch. "Shall we stop?" she asked calmly. Rolen froze, then shook his head. "Good. Then keep your hands on the table."

Who the hell does she think she is? Rolen snarled inwardly. But his hands, he realized, remained where they were.

Her eyes softened with pleasure, and she reached for the breast that Kantou wasn't licking, drawing her fingers slowly over it while holding Rolen's gaze. Rolen gritted his teeth. He could feel his balls swelling, pressing against the chair. Surreptitiously, he rocked, increasing the pressure. He saw Soleyla frown and drop her hand.

She rose fluidly, moving to stand behind him. Her hands slid across Rolen's shoulders, caressing them, then down his chest. His nipples tingled as she brushed them lightly. "Do you like that, Rolen?"

He didn't answer. But his cock, straining at his breechclout, answered for him.

She chuckled, deep in her throat. The sound sent a shiver down his spine.

"You must learn to answer when I ask you a question." Rolen jerked forward, out of her grasp, but she grabbed his hair and pulled him back. Rage shot through him.

"Let me go!"

"As you wish."

He felt himself released, and she moved back to her chair, settling in it demurely. Kantou curled again by her feet, seemingly content. She lifted her wineglass and reached for the food. "So tell me, what sort of crops do you grow on this planet?"

What? His cock was so hard he was afraid he might pass out, and she wanted to discuss *agriculture?* Rolen ground his jaw, feeling his balls pulse with unreleased cum. He should just throw them out, call in one of the women and have her service him properly, damn it!

"As Kantou services me?"

Rolen glared, shocked. Did the bitch read minds, too?

"You were muttering," she replied. "Have you no will at all? You can't even control when you speak or not."

He swore soundly.

She smiled, amused. "Look at Kantou. See how perfectly he waits, how still, how controlled. Do you think that is easy, Rolen? Could you do it?"

Before he could retort, she spoke again. "Kantou."

Kantou moved, and Rolen could see he was still utterly hard, the veins pulsing in his cock. But his face was calm.

How did he do it? Rolen wondered. That enormous erection, begging to be stroked . . . He himself was nothing like under-endowed, but the sight of that massive cock left him speechless. He couldn't look away as Kantou, under his lady's orders, knelt between her legs, his tongue moving eagerly between her folds. Rolen remembered the salty taste of her, the way her hands had buried themselves in his hair, drawing him to her, and groaned.

She looked at him, smiled, and spread her legs wider, giving him an unimpeded view.

He felt as if he'd become nothing but eyes and cock. He watched every flick of Kantou's tongue, watched her eyes half-close in pleasure as he suckled her clit, stared ravenously at her hands caressing her own breasts. Her eyes met his as she tweaked her nipples between her fingers, tugging on them. Then she pinched them, fiercely, and gasped with pleasure. Rolen felt a wave of agony shoot down his spine. He could barely sit still, barely keep his hands off himself . . .

Yet if he didn't, she would stop.

Soleyla smiled. "Rolen," she said, and beckoned lazily. He rose, his cock straining from his clout. "Take that off," she commanded. He shed it hurriedly. "Now, come here."

He did, kneeling down at her gesture. She studied his erection, considering. It was thick, if not as long as Kantou's, the head swollen and purple, aching to be touched. "No," she said as his hand automatically moved toward it. "I doubt your control. Kantou."

Rolen froze as Kantou's hand closed around his shaft, applying pressure, but not moving. Horrified, Rolen felt an urge to rock himself against that grip. He wanted nothing more than to come in this man's hand.

Soleyla smiled. "Rub him gently, Kantou. Do not let him come. And you," she continued to Rolen, "you will suck my breast."

Grabbing his hair, she yanked his head to her. Blindly, he drew her nipple between his lips, mouthing it hungrily, hearing her small sighs of pleasure as he suckled. "Harder," she commanded, and he complied. Kantou's hand moved on his cock, so slow it was excruciating, and yet the very agony made it harder still. He felt frozen, pinned between hand and breast, an empty slate for her desire to write itself upon. He wanted more, and more, and wanted it never to end.

He opened his eyes and saw Kantou's mouth pulling at her other nipple. Like twins they nestled at her breasts, as she arched her back and thrust those beautiful tits into their greedy, tugging mouths. Almost unconsciously, Rolen reached out, feeling Kantou's cock slide into his grasp. He glanced up at Soleyla, and she smiled down indulgently.

Wrapping his fingers around the velvety shaft, Rolen worked his hand up and down, in time with Kantou's strokes on his own cock. Cautiously, he increased the pressure, and felt Kantou's hand clamp harder around him as well. He could feel his balls swelling, pressing against his thighs, aching with the load building up inside them.

"Enough!" Soleyla cried. They sat back immediately, dropping their hands meekly to their sides. Rolen stared at the man kneeling across from him in shock. God, how had she done this to him, and so quickly? She spoke, and he obeyed — and, he realized, he *wanted* her to command him.

At the wicked gleam in her eye, he suspected he was going to find out exactly how deep that want ran.

"You said something earlier, Rolen."

"My lady?"

Sweet God, had he really just said those words?

Her mouth curved like a cat's. "You said you didn't see how I could fuck Kantou. I think it's time to show you. Kantou."

Obediently, Kantou turned, presenting his ass to her. He leaned forward, arching his back, and Rolen was shocked at the lust that flared through him at the sight of that high, vulnerable ass. He watched, almost panting, as Soleyla licked her fingers and worked the moisture over Kantou's tight hole, which gaped slightly in anticipation.

"Do you like that, Kantou?"

"Yes, my lady."

"Do you want more?"

Kantou answered with a groan.

Soleyla reached forward, snagged the small pitcher of oil off the table, and drizzled it lovingly over his cheeks. She caressed them, spreading the oil so his entire ass gleamed in the lamplight, then pushed his cheeks apart, clearly revealing the tight pink hole between them.

Rolen stared, fascinated, as the muscles around it quivered, gaping and contracting, wanting something inside it. He felt his own sphincter pulse in response, sending shockwaves of desire up his cock.

Soleyla whispered, "Tell me what you want, Kantou."

"Oh, lady," he breathed, "I want you to fuck me. I want you to shove yourself inside of me. I want you to pound my ass. I want you to split me so wide open it makes me scream."

Rolen's cock was so swollen he could barely think.

Soleyla glanced at him sidelong. "Would you like to see how I fuck him?"

He nodded mutely, feeling saliva flood his mouth. She wrapped her hand around his shaft, her palm slick with oil, and slid it, up, down. *I could come*, he thought incoherently, *right now.*

She tugged on it gently, pulling him forward, and positioned him between Kantou's legs so that his bulging cockhead nudged Kantou's asshole. Rolen tilted his head back, swallowing, as he heard Kantou whimper in longing. Soleyla knelt behind him, her arms around his waist, and whispered in his ear, "This is how I fuck my Kantou."

Slowly, her hand firmly gripping his shaft, she worked the head of his cock into Kantou's hole.

Rolen heard her breathing grow hoarse as Kantou's sphincter spread, enveloping him. God, it was so tight! He wanted to plunge in, shove himself deep into it, but Soleyla held him there, his cockhead barely inside that hot, hungry ass, allowing Kantou time to adjust to his size. Rolen could feel the tight ring of muscle pulsing just under the rim of his cockhead, and bit down on his lip, struggling not to come. Slowly, the pulsing sensation eased, and Soleyla pushed on his hips, rocking him forward gently, smoothly, until he was encased in

Kantou up to the hilt.

Rolen leaned against him, feeling his pubic bone pressed against Kantou's ass-cheeks, not daring to move. If he moved, he would come.

Sensation flooded through him, draining him of reason, of will, of everything but the need to hold himself still. He felt Soleyla behind him, leaning against his back, her weight pushing him steadily deeper, deeper. Kantou strained back against him, impaling himself on Rolen's shaft, hungry for every last inch of his cock.

"Do you like that, Kantou?"

"Yes," he hissed as he slowly, slowly rocked himself forward.

Rolen could feel that ring of tight muscle dragging down his shaft, and he clenched his jaw. Then Kantou thrust backward, driving him home, and Rolen's head snapped back with the fire that burned through him.

He fought it, held onto it, and climbed to another level. The ecstasy diminished not at all, but became manageable, bearable. Which was good because Soleyla was now pulling his hips back, then shoving them forward, using his cock to fuck her beloved Kantou, faster and faster. Kantou squirmed below him, arching his back, whimpering, "Fuck me, oh fuck me. Harder! Please, harder!" Rolen pounded his ass, his balls smashed between them, burying himself in that hot, tight, slick tunnel. He couldn't stop, he couldn't control the need to keep thrusting himself, harder and harder, spurred on by Kantou's ecstatic cries and Soleyla's breath in his ear . . .

"Stop!" she commanded, and it was Rolen's turn to whimper as he froze, his cock pulsing in time with his heartbeat. Slowly, gently, she pulled his hips back. His engorged cockhead slid out of Kantou with a small, audible pop.

"Now it's your turn," she whispered as Kantou turned toward them. Rolen eyed Kantou's enormous shaft, straining into the air. She wasn't really going to . . . He swallowed nervously.

Soleyla smiled and rose to her feet. "Kantou, prepare him."

He felt himself bent over, his hips resting on the seat of the chair, and his asscheeks spread wide as Soleyla moved around the tent, shifting things. Kantou's fingers probed at his hole, dabbing it with oil. He groaned. This was unthinkable! No man let himself be used in this way. But his cock thundered with need, and he felt an overwhelming ache above and behind his balls, an emptiness, a longing. The fingers pressed gently against his tight muscle, lubricating it, loosening it. It was almost like a doorway, one that had to be opened to reach the ecstasy on the far side. He heard himself moan low in his throat, yearning.

Soleyla returned. He looked up, almost frightened, and was relieved to see a candle in her hands. She knelt behind him, her strong hands on his ass, and slowly inserted the tapered tip. He closed his eyes, feeling the muscle stretch, then a cool, soothing wetness as she drizzled more oil. "Kantou," she whispered, and apparently motioned as well, for Rolen heard Kantou rise, come around in front of him, and kneel. Soleyla leaned over him, playing just the tip of the candle teasingly in and out of his hole, and whispered, "So tell me, Rolen, do you want this?"

"Yes," he hissed, feeling his balls contract with need.

"Will you do anything I tell you?"

He gritted his teeth, but his groan betrayed him. He wanted to do whatever she told him, but it was impossible to admit that, not out loud.

It would *have* to be possible. She slid the candle deeper, just an inch, just enough to make him feel how badly he wanted it inside him.

"Tell me."

"Anything. Anything you want!" *Bitch*, he added silently.

"Do you want me to fuck you?"

There was no pleasing the woman! She demanded it all, his pride, his obedience. His *willingness*. "Yes."

"Tell me."

"Yes, damn it! I want you to fuck me!"

"Hard?"

"Oh, God, yes. Hard. So hard it hurts. Please." He felt his muscles twitching, realized he was shoving his ass back at her, begging her for it, begging her to enter him, plunder him.

He could almost see her smile as she leaned forward, whispering, "And while I do, you shall pleasure Kantou."

He shut his eyes tight. This couldn't be happening. It couldn't possibly feel this good. But the sensations that racked him made every other experience he'd ever had pale in comparison. He wanted her to use him, enter him, *fuck* him. He felt warm flesh pressing against his lips, opened them, felt his jaw forced wider as Kantou slid the tip of his cock into his wet, waiting mouth.

Rolen ran his tongue over it, amazed at its smoothness, delighting himself in poking the slit over and over. He felt Kantou shudder and took him deeper in response. Kantou groaned, and Rolen felt a rush of power he'd never before experienced. To bring another man to senseless, uncontrollable lust! He wrapped his lips around the rim of Kantou's cockhead, sucked it, hard—and felt Soleyla penetrate his ass.

The candle was smooth and hard, just thick enough to make him hunger for more. He arched his back, sending it deeper into him, felt her slide it smoothly back and forth, each time a little further. It was as if there was a button somewhere deep inside that tight tunnel, and he needed her to press it, needed her to shove the candle all the way inside him. Tilting his hips, he spurred her on, feeling her slam it in as he moaned in delight, his mouth full of cock.

His own shaft throbbed against the chair as he rocked back

and forth, feeling Kantou slide in and out of his mouth as Soleyla fucked him. Rolen felt her hands on his hips, shoving them downward, increasing the pressure where his shaft ground against the chair. Groping, he reached out, found Kantou's balls, heard him groan in mingled agony and lust as Rolen played with them, tugging the skin, feeling their weight. Rolen pulled Kantou forward, burying him deep in his mouth, felt his tongue drop down as Kantou entered his throat, stretching it wide. His own balls ached, and he whimpered, shifting his ass. Soleyla sensed his need and reached her hand under to grab them, squeezing them tight.

"More?"

He nodded hungrily, his mouth stretched wide around Kantou's cock, and she clamped his balls hard, sending fire running through him.

"Do you like him sucking your cock, Kantou?"

Kantou groaned and thrust harder. Rolen could feel his balls tightening, and prayed she would not make them stop.

"Fuck his mouth, Kantou. Fuck it hard."

Kantou lunged his hips forward, choking Rolen, pistoning himself between Rolen's stretched, aching lips. He felt his own orgasm gathering, roaring like wildfire under the pressure in his ass. He understood now why Kantou knelt so meekly at this woman's feet. It was ecstasy to serve her, to fulfill her every whim. And she repaid that servility with delirious bliss.

His ass was suddenly abandoned, and he whined in longing, then surrendered joyously as he felt her turn the candle around, forcing the thicker base of it into his ass. It felt huge inside him, filling him in a way he'd never imagined. His balls spasmed, leaking a first spurt of cum onto the chair. He slid through the slickness of his own juices, insane with need.

Kantou buried his hands in Rolen's hair, yanking it hard as he rammed himself deeper. His huge balls contracted under

Rolen's teasing fingers, and cum flooded Rolen's mouth, hot, sticky, delicious. He moaned, sucking harder as Kantou's cock jerked in his throat, plunging deeper, savaging him in the frenzy of orgasm.

Rolen thrust his ass back, forcing the candle all the way in. It impaled him, splitting him open. Soleyla shoved her hips behind it, grinding it in. She rocked against him, faster, faster, working her clit against his tailbone. He could hear her harsh breathing, and felt her fingers clamp convulsively on his balls. She shuddered behind him, ramming her hips forward, jamming the candle deeper into his ass. His tunnel quivered around it, squeezing and contracting as his balls tightened in her punishing grip and cum spurted from his throbbing cock in endless, white-hot waves.

Later, they lay in Rolen's huge bed. Soleyla had one arm loosely draped around each of them, enjoying the weight of their two heads resting, one on each shoulder. *Yes*, she thought. *This is how it should be. Delight given freely, taken with joy, not forced or withheld by laws or fears or custom.*

And if it took a war to make her mother see that? *Then,* Soleyla promised herself, *a war we will have.*

She was Soleyla Devarian, Guardian captain and daughter of the First Senator of the Nine-Star League. She did not make promises lightly.

"Rolen."

"My lady?"

She smiled triumphantly into the darkness. "Did you like that, my darling?"

On her other side, Kantou shifted restlessly. Jealous? No, that was silly. Surely Kantou must know how she felt about him. She stroked his beautiful, long, soft brown hair as she waited for Rolen's answer.

"No, my lady."

"No?" She turned her head, surprised, and glanced down at the massive man curled submissively beside her.

"No. I loved it."

Soleyla smiled and looked down at those two bowed heads, ash-brown and black as pitch, mere inches from her breasts. She felt a familiar heat blossom between her thighs at the sight.

"So tell me, Rolen, should we do it again?"

Devarian Uprising

Devarian Chronicles: 2

Captain Soleyla Devarian must defy both her loyalties and her mother—the powerful and brutal Rachel Devarian, First Senator of the Nine-Star League—to help Rolen and the Antoreans in their rebellion. But in her devotion to Rolen's cause, will Soleyla lose her beloved Kantou?

Available on April 7, 2023, at Extasy Books and all major book sellers.

ABOUT SIERRA DAFOE

Sierra Dafoe has a thing for hot romantic heroes, cool ocean breezes, and — of all things — chickens. The day she figures out how to keep livestock on a sailboat, she's moving to the Caribbean.

An award-winning author who garnered three CAPA nominations in her first year of publishing, Sierra has gone on to receive numerous awards and recommended reads for her work. Her home on the web is sierradafoe.com, where you can find excerpts, sneak peeks, and all her latest news. Sign up for her newsletter for a special monthly contest!

www.ingramcontent.com/pod-product-compliance
Lightning Source LLC
Chambersburg PA
CBHW070225140626
46555CB00018B/1310